NOWHERE

NOVELS BY THOMAS BERGER

Little Big Man (1964)
Killing Time (1967)
Regiment of Women (1973)
Sneaky People (1975)
Arthur Rex (1978)
Neighbors (1980)
The Feud (1983)

The Reinhart Series
Crazy in Berlin (1958)
Reinhart in Love (1962)
Vital Parts (1970)
Reinhart's Women (1981)

Russel Wren, Private Investigator
Who Is Teddy Villanova? (1977)
Nowhere (1985)

NOWHERE

THOMAS BERGER

DELTA/SEYMOUR LAWRENCE

Published by
Dell Publishing Co., Inc.
1 Dag Hammarskjold Plaza
New York, New York 10017

For information address: Delacorte Press/Seymour Lawrence
New York, New York.
Delta ® TM 755118, Dell Publishing Co., Inc.

ISBN: 0-385-29464-6

Reprinted by arrangement with Delacorte Press/Seymour Lawrence

Printed in the United States of America

October 1986

10 9 8 7 6 5 4 3 2 1

To Guy Davenport

NOWHERE

1

My name has always been Russel Wren. My game, off and on, is private investigation. In recent years divorce had fallen off. Amongst the people who have sufficient funds to hire a spouse-spy, the kind of trends that applaud novelties in sexual behavior had done its work: adultery became too shamefully banal to cite in legal procedures, and I drew the line at finding evidence of necrophilia or, for that matter, urolagnia.

Fortunately for me, however (though no doubt deplorable for the commonweal—but one example of how interests can naturally conflict in the traffic of humankind), the incidence of shoplifting and employee pilfering had increased greatly as the years went by, and in retail business it was the rare shop that was not threatened with being wishboned between the unscrupulous public and its own thieving clerks.

Posing as a surly wino, a type that ranges with complete impunity in New York, as a raving madman does amongst the Bedouin, I collapsed in a corner of Ben Rothman's delicatessen and in the course of six hours, peeping through a hole in my battered fedora (under which I pretended to snore), I saw one of his white-aproned employees persistently ring up NO SALE while exchanging foodstuffs for money. "Big fellow?" asked Ben, having heard my report. "Sandy hair? Mustache? My own son! Naw, s'all right. Else I'd have to raise his salary!"

I had also observed considerable shoplifting. Rothman, like most white merchants, disregarded all plunder by any person of swarthy hue (indeed, I suspect that more than one extravagantly suntanned Caucasian seized the chance so offered), but there were white thieves aplenty, both male and female, and not one was ill dressed.

By prearranged signal I indicated these perpetrators to Rothman at his post behind the meat counter. He did nothing at the time, but after hours he identified them to me as, every one, his regular customers and mostly from the professional classes, for example, his own ophthalmologist.

My labors having led to no usable ends, I feared that Ben might reject his obligation to pay my fee, but he did not. What he did was to suggest that I collect its equivalent, retail value, in merchandise from his shelves—furtively.

"You don't mean shoplift?" I asked.

"Do me a favor," said Rothman. "I'll claim it on the insurance."

Simultaneously we ran the gamut of Manhattan sign language—raised eyebrows and weary shrug—and I proceeded stoically to fill my pockets with cans of boned turkey, jars of macadamia nuts, and frozen yoghurt Good Humors—the last a taste I had acquired from my former secretary and brief roommate Peggy Tumulty, who during the week we lived together subsisted exclusively on this confection, preceded by either egg-drop soup from a Chinese takeout assembly line or packages of fried pork rinds, washed down with a cola sans sugar, caffeine, or taste, the cute TV commercials for which temporarily rinsed her palate of a yen for any other fluid.

Our relationship reached a natural end at just about the point at which she was ready to assume another fad in food. I had had other female friends before, and I had some after, but I am naturally, even notoriously, a loner. Nor did I replace Peggy. Not only was economy necessary for me (the Rothmans were few and far between), but it seemed to be generally in good taste, which statement is prefatory to my confession that at the moment of which I write I was living in my new office. Thank me for not saying "orifice," given its size: one room.

My former chambers had been situated in a building that was torn down two years earlier and replaced with an automated garage (which, incidentally, when I had last passed it, was itself already marked for demolition: a sign asked passersby to watch for the new home of some state agency working for the abolition of envy, offering free psychiatric treatment for any citizen not yet a millionaire).

My new place of business and temporary abode was not far from my old one: like all wild animals (and most human whores for that matter), I am bound to my turf by invisible cords. Unless the motive is merely a lack of wonder, this might be called a sense of place. Whatever, I am habituated to the area; its vapors are not alien to my snout (whereas I sneeze at the beach); even its derelicts have their place in my maintenance of a state of well-being, and if a regular is missing I might begin, in terror, to question whether even God's where He belongs.

So on this shank of an evening in June. Before my time (he told me) Rothman stayed open all night. When I first came to the neighborhood in the mid-1970's he did business till midnight. Each year saw the deli close an hour earlier. Persons now in their tender years might grow up to buy breakfast there and nothing else.

I moved along Twenty-third Street in my wino disguise. Consequently I walked in peace. That there is no effective form of defense against a derelict is an irreducible truth of city life.

However, as I passed the post office I was hailed by some of the figures slumped there in the embrasures of the several front doors with which the clairvoyant architects of the Depression Era had anticipated the needs of generations hence. Why I felt an obligation to respond I cannot explain, unless it was to test my disguise against the inspection of professionals.

"Will you buy my birthright for a pint of message?" This question was put by a man whose mouth I could not discern, what with the shadows, the whiskers, and a stocking cap that was apparently pulled down to his clavicles. Then I realized that he was wearing no cap: what had seemed a coarse-textured yarn was actually his face.

He had called my bluff. I saw no decent way to rise above this but by crossing his palm with coin of the realm—more than half that sentence is a direct quote from him. For some reason shopworn phrases take on a new sheen for me when produced by a bum.

I rounded the corner into lower Lex. My office was nearby, one floor up, over a ground-level establishment that had changed its identity every few weeks since I assumed residence, from tobacco shop to souvlaki stand to emporium for obscene books. But all of these establishments had failed soon enough, and next came a pair of twin brothers with unidentifiable accents, who opened a restaurant called, *sic*, La Table Français, but as I discovered upon the occasion of my first lunch there, the pâté was common liverwurst and the *poularde à la reine en croûte* was a dead ringer for Swanson's chicken pot pie (and they had insolently left mine in its original plate of foil). This meal was priced at $39.95, and the tines of my fork were webbed with dried egg—which on application the waiter genially chipped away with a sable thumbnail before wiping the implement on his shiny-trousered ham and replacing it in my fingers.

Yet this eatery was manifestly an enormous success, perhaps because of the enthusiastic reviews it evoked from all the local food critics, one of whom gave it five of his little honorific symbols, the spatula-and-pancake, and it was routine to see, as I did now, prosperous-looking clients waiting humbly for a table in the long queue that reached the sidewalk.

The striped canopy, which extended overhead from door to curbside support-pipes, gave some protection from the rain when it came, but none from human menaces, and there was no paucity of these in the neighborhood. Having been spotted as an impostor by the post-office lot and having paid for it, I forgot my disguise as I passed the restaurant, en route to my adjacent door. But the last customer in the queue, a portly soul with fluffy cotton-wool sideburns, in the poltroonish belief that I was about to put the bite on him or else vomit on his shoes (which incidentally were of burgundy-colored patent leather, with a horse brass at the tongue), tendered me a crumpled dollar bill. I confess I accepted it, touched my hatbrim, called him "Cap," ambled the few steps to my own entrance, and darted in.

Between Lumpenproletarian and Conspicuous Consumer (who bracket New York) I had emerged seventy-five cents to the good! I was smiling over this unprecedented profit of the man-in-the-middle as I groped my way through the unlighted vestibule, which smelled of mammal (perhaps even primate) ordure, found my key to the inner door, and opened it. I climbed the splintery staircase in the murky light of a bulb of the lowest wattage. My sense of well-being had pretty well run its course by the time I reached the upper landing—and even so had been unusually long-lived.

But unlike some of my fellow men I never wondered what I was doing in New York. For years, you see, I had been writing a play, and there was but one Broadway in all the world. Call me sentimental, but I still get a lump in my throat when I see stars in my eyes—

Metaphor of masochism! I was savagely assaulted at the top of the stair. It would be humiliating to report that my attackers were small children, none of whom I suppose was older than eight or nine, had there not been two score of them, and for viciousness there is probably little to choose between one shark and fifty piranhas. I suppose I might as well add that they were all girls. I soon discovered that, no doubt owing to my education in the liberal arts, I could not defend myself against female minors. (It might have been a different story had I been attacked by a gang of male Army majors!) I was told repeatedly, in terms of which the clarity was no doubt enhanced by the obscenity, that their restraint would not be eternal, that to ensure my life I should do well not only to surrender my money but also to be so good as to open the door of my office, saving them the trouble of smashing it in.

Once again my derelict's disguise had failed to deceive. I was tempted to debate with these youngsters, but a good many of them brandished edged weapons to reinforce their argument. Therefore I produced my wallet, which was instantly torn away and seemingly eaten. I suppose I had had all of eighteen, twenty dollars therein. With foresight I had some time before discontinued the carrying of identifying documents on my person: no harm could be done by their lack (in New York proving one's existence is futile), whereas they could easily be lost to pickpockets and such assailants as I now faced.

But these small girls were not an unruly mob of amateurs. My money proved contemptible to them. They wanted credit cards, driver's license, and Social Security tickets, and the like, in all of which there was a lucrative resale trade. Finding nothing beyond the few miserable bills but a supply of my business cards (which futhermore they could not read), they now appeared to be on the verge of declaring me useless—an ominous declaration when arrived at with regard to a helpless enemy.

I suspect I should not now be writing this account had not the bulb on the landing burned out at that moment. In the darkness I managed to thrust myself against the wall and feel my way along to the door and by touch locate the several locks, but identifying the proper key for each except by sight was the work of many moments, and in truth I escaped recapture only because these youngsters believed the light had gone out by reason of another general blackout and they were eager to get to the nearest five-and-ten and sack it.

After hearing the rush downstairs and the silence that succeeded it, I counted slowly to fifty to be on the side of prudence, and then to still another fifty in the name of pusillanimity. Then I got my locks open and, as a man will by habit, threw the light switch up, even though I, too, supposed the power failure universal.

But the bulb came on with what could be called at least a modest burst of glory, given my late trial in the darkness. I seized it fondly by the neck (this acrobat hangs, headfirst, from the ceiling), and plugged into its auxiliary socket the cord that heats my hotplate. I put a pint of Jackrabbit spring water, from its gallon jug, into my teakettle and set it on to boil, which it would surely do within the hour.

I poured myself a brimful of Uncle Tito's Family Rosé in an ex-jam glass. My desk was also my dining table. I snapped a folded rectangle of oysterish oilcloth from the lowest drawer and spread it across the board. I set in place a plastic plate from Lamston's, flanked by miniature cutlery that had once flown the friendly skies of United. A paper napkin, from a supply that I replenished whenever I visited a lunch counter, completed the setting.

I emptied my pockets of the fee for the Rothman job and put the cans, jars, bottles, and packages before me. The frozen yoghurt bars had begun to thaw in my pocket, I'm afraid. A bad choice: I had no refrigeration on the premises. An evil thought came to me: I could open the front window and drop this mess on the helpless persons waiting on the sidewalk for entrance to the restaurant. Such revenge-fantasies come easily in New York and usually involve innocent victims who bear no responsibility for one's plight.

I resisted this impulse (which was more than the swine could say who launched a half-filled cole-slaw container at me from a fourth-floor window in the Garment District a fortnight earlier), and I emptied that pocket into my wastecan and changed into a pair of corduroy jeans. With a letter opener and a paperweight I succeeded in breaching the various containers in my collection, and I supped on Danish Camembert, anchovy-caper coils, Diet Biscottes, cocktail meatballs, tinned kippers, and chestnut puree, to mention only a few of the dishes, and eventually the kettle steamed and I was able to brew, from a powdered mix, in my only mug without a hairline crack, a sort of coffee flavored with synthetic pineapple and molasses: once a favorite refreshment, if the label could be believed, at the Hapsburg Court in Old Vienna.

Having fed, I sluiced my palate with the last of the rosé, gathered the containers and crumbs into a plastic bag from a supply I had filched from a roll at some supermarket produce counter, opened my rear window, and airmailed the garbage into the cavity between my building and that which faced on Madison Square, into which areaway I confess I had never actually looked since I moved in. I must say that this mode of rubbish disposal had been suggested—nay, demanded—by the super of this decaying edifice, who came around but once a fortnight except in case of emergency (at which time he could not be found at all) and the day before Xmas (when *I* hid from *him*, for once, and was not even flushed from concealment by the lighted cigar he furiously, recklessly, hurled through my transom).

I put away my tablecloth and from a neighboring drawer of the desk took out the script of my play. Perhaps this would be the night on which I should lick the problem of the third act, always a ticklish one for the dramatist, especially if like me he had filled the preceding two-thirds with insoluble problems, such as that of the priest who does not discover his horror of women until he leaves the Church to marry a Jewess with whose sociopolitical ideology he is in sympathy: a sort of radical bourgeoisism in which all citizens are compelled by law to marry and produce one child of each sex and to travel a sufficient distance by Winnebago camper each summer, else be placed at hard labor in regional work camps. Obviously I had an axe to grind, but I did not want to be so flagrant as to offend future theater parties.

I thought of making the girl black—or perhaps the priest. Or the priest might rather be made a rabbi, a black rabbi. No, an Episcopalian priest, a female Episcopalian, who is furthermore gay, and her mate is a black woman . . . no, I was getting too sentimental now. I must start all over again, my hero an honest, hearty farmer of Swedish extraction; he comes to the big city; he meets a kindly female impressionist; he—

At this point my telephone rang, somewhere beneath the tangle of bedclothes on the studio couch. If the truth be known, I was relieved, though (presumably to impress myself, in the absence of any other human beings) I slammed down my Bic Banana, cursed, and assumed an expression of creativity annoyingly interrupted. But not being sufficiently prosperous to impose this upon the world, I answered genially.

A bass and I should say utterly humorless voice told me: "Joo batter get out from zis house, my fran', or be destroyed."

I confess I was distracted by the accent, which seemed to have elements of many languages not closely related to one another. I decided it was a hoax: such things are commonplace in my profession. Many wags enjoy pulling the leg of a private investigator. Call it thrill-seeking, but there are people who apparently get pleasure from calling a total stranger and, in a ridiculously incredible falsetto, making him an indecent proposal. Usually I drop the handpiece in silence, but on this evening I was piqued.

"Drop dead, you jerk," I growled, borrowing the taxi-driver's idiom, which is useful when one is feeling as verbally uninspired as I was at that moment.

"Is nawt time for little games, fallow, I assure you. Bums are there!"

I sniffed. "If you are serious, my friend, then I must assure you that the bums in this neighborhood wouldn't, *couldn't*, destroy anybody. They are far too feeble." Still, I didn't much like the news that some of them had again bedded down inside the front door: that entryway stank enough as it was.

"Dun't talk like a prrrick," said the voice, with lip-trilled, not uvular, *r.* "I can tell you zis: bums will go off in tan minutes. You must live or die." Or perhaps it was "leave or die." Either way, it was at this point that I first began to grasp what he was trying to tell me. Though funnily enough I was still slow to reach worry.

"Ah," I said patiently, "you mean 'bombs,' don't you? Things that blow up? Uh-huh. Say, would you be offended if I asked—" I was interested in identifying his native tongue, but since this sort of inquiry might offend, I decided to add some soft soap: "Not that I'm suggesting you don't speak English well."

"You crazy fokker!" he shouted. "Get your ahss from out that house or lose it! Now don't talk no more, just ron." He added what seemed a total irrelevancy: "Sebastiani Liberation Front." And hung up abruptly.

Trends come and go in all eras, but I should say that only in ours do they get successively more vile: in recent years it had become fashionable to detonate explosives in public places in the name of some usually unrecognizable cause. Frankly, I think the urge to destroy comes first, and then he who has it looks for a slogan to mouth while blowing up people and things, with the idea that his mayhem thereby becomes perfectly reasonable.

At the moment I did not require a precise identification of the caller's group: I had wasted too much time already. I dropped the phone and, I think, was out the door before I heard it hit the desk. I took the stairs in two bounds and was in the street on the third.

A short, redhaired daughter of joy, a regular on the beat, was just sauntering past the building. "Hi, Rus!" said she. (I sometimes exchanged a bit of chaff with these ladies.) "You don't look like you got it on straight, if you don't mind me saying so."

It is with some pride that I can report my unthinking response as gallant: I swept this (fortunately little) tart up off her feet and, carrying her in the crook of my arm, like an outsized loaf of bread, I gained most of the block to the south before the explosion came, destroying not only my building but also the restaurant next door and the liquor shop across the street, along with its companions, the Asiatic spice shop and the shallow doorway of the *hôtel de passe* of which my current burden, the petite harlot, was a relentless customer if she could find a series of live ones. And of course all windows were shattered for a quarter of a mile by the punch of sound.

Being at a right angle to the blast, and a street away, we suffered only the bruises sustained in the plunge to the street I took owing to the aural shock. Which Bobbie, for such was her name, had the effrontery to chide me for!

"Chrissakes, Rus," she sibilated indignantly, hopping to her feet and brushing at the scuffed buttock of her designer jeans, which incidentally she wore a good deal more modestly than did most current females who were freebies.

"So don't thank me for saving your life!" I said. I was still sitting in the middle of the sidewalk, looking towards Twenty-third Street. I had not yet made the foregoing list of casualty-buildings. Indeed, for a moment or two I was enjoying the odd serenity that claims me on the very threshold of total collapse. I could reflect gratefully that while the Whatever Liberation Front were thoroughgoing swine to plant that bomb, I could not hate them for warning me, in fact demanding that I leave the premises. I could only assume that if the restaurant were still occupied, a similar call had been placed next door, and to whoever was available in the other buildings.

Still breathing deeply from my exertion, though otherwise, so far as I was aware, in standard condition (which is to say, at thirty-five somewhat flabby though underweight; hair, teeth, and eyes OK)—I am holding back the narrative here, because I have always been fascinated by the tendency of reality to be amateurishly timed.

Meanwhile, various persons came running towards the locus of the explosion, from up or down Lex and out of the numbered side streets. Bobbie was sufficiently eager for business, owing no doubt to her exigent pimp, to solicit several of the males in the collecting crowd, and in fact she finally netted a chap with a gray mustache and tinted eyeglasses, who led her to a double-parked Chrysler Imperial whose engine was idling and whose plates had been issued by the state of New Jersey.

Eventually, though in reality it was probably all of twenty seconds, I got to my feet, remembering to hope that I had not fallen into the dog dirt that was once again extant, now that the population had become blasé about the poop-scoop ordinance, and finding none on a finger-search of my clothing, I approached my late office-*cum*-home, much of which was no doubt represented now in the pile of rubbish that filled the street. But more, in fact most, as I could see when the angle permitted, had plunged to the lower portion of the building, and had been followed by the roof and the furnishings thereof: vanes and vents and great slices of the surface of Tar Beach. The jagged walls of the first three stories contained all that had stood above and made a kind of giant topless box of rubbish.

Somewhere in the thick of things was the play on which I had heroically labored for so long, without, however, having had the sense to make an extra copy of it for preservation in a safe place.

On the other hand, one might profitably see this experience as the opportunity for a new beginning, and in truth nobody had ever seemed to cotton to that now buried work even as an idea—even when sitting drunk on the next bar stool (having got there on my money) in my local, a Third Avenue establishment frequented by people who fancy themselves as belonging to the intelligentsia because they can often name the principal players in prewar movies, follow pro football, and drink less hard liquor than any previous generation.

The police cars began to arrive; and the fire department, in many companies and with much apparatus, clanged in from all points. Before I could collect my wits (which of course had been badly jostled), such a crowd of professionals and amateurs of disaster had collected that I found it difficult to report to anyone in authority.

"Would you let me through?" I asked a beefy, beery man who had apparently come from the Hibernian bar a block or so north: he still clutched his glass of foam.

"Naw," he genially replied. "I was here first, pal."

"But I *lived* in there," I protested.

"Call that living?" He remained rooted.

I abandoned this fruitless colloquy when a cop came through the nearby crowd.

"Officer!" I cried. "That was my home, where the bomb went off!"

But he, too, was indifferent and pushed me aside with the heavy and, I always suspect, mocking courtesy of the New York police officer. "*Exkewse* me. Hey. Awright. Lemme. OK, folks. Huh? Naw. Yeah?" So far as I could hear, though they seemed to cover every eventuality, none of these noises was made in actual response to anything said by anybody else.

I tried another cop or two, with no better success, but then, seeing some television newspeople arrive and emerge from their vans with hand-held cameras and lights, I decided to make application in that quarter, and maneuvered myself through the crowd until I confronted Jackie Johansen, a local channel's sob sister, easily recognizable but in person displaying a graininess of cheek and lifelessness of bleached hair not evident on the home screen.

"Jackie!" said I. "I'm the man concerned. It was my home that was bombed. You've got an exclusive interview!"

She stared briefly at me with her pale eyes, and then turned to one of the males in her entourage, a short, very hairy, clipboard-holding man in worn denims and Nike shoes, and asked: "Who the fuck is this?"

"A nothing, a schmuck," said he, thrusting into the crowd, breaking a route for Jackie and a lithe fellow toting a camera. They vanished.

"Ah, humanity!" sighed someone to my right. I turned and saw a derelict whose discolored skin and blue teeth looked vaguely familiar: he had been amongst the lot on the steps of the post office when I came home only—what?—an hour or two ago. Now I had no home. Foul as he was, I had an impulse to hurl myself on his malodorous chest and cry my eyes out—but this was gone in an instant. I grimaced and headed away from the crowd.

But this embarrassing acquaintance was relentless! He stayed on my heels, moving remarkably nimbly for a wino, crying outmoded historical banalities, which for some reason annoyed me more at this moment than obscenities would have: " 'Man is a political animal.' . . . 'Power tends to corrupt.' . . . 'A little rebellion now and then is a good thing.' "

I'm afraid that all I could think of at this juncture was the feeble " 'Let 'em eat cake.' " I hustled on towards Third Avenue, having no destination in mind, but was soon stopped by a jeer.

"That's *'Qu'ils mangent de la brioche,'* " shouted the bum. "Not *gâteau,* nor was it said by Marie Antoinette!"

I was stung by this gibe. I turned slowly, ransacking my brain for something, anything, that could be launched as a Parthian shot.

But before I managed to make a sound, my tormentor came close to me and said, in a quiet but authoritative voice, as contrasted to his derelict's bombast: "Follow me. I'm one of Them."

I don't know why, but I trusted him, probably on the mere strength of his scholarly pretensions, to be at least more than a common bum. He pushed, as if drunkenly, past me, maintaining the imposture, and lurched to the corner of Third. I came along behind. The avenue was deserted, all of local humanity being over at the site of the blast on Lex. My man staggered to the curb and stepped down into the gutter between a parked VW Beetle and a large, battered gray van, where, hands at his crotch, he was seemingly preparing to urinate but was actually checking discreetly on the clearness of the coast; having determined which to be acceptable, he scratched at the door of the van. One of its panels soon opened, and he stepped up and in, and I followed suit.

During the few instants before the door was closed it was dark in there, and I could not so much as see who had let us in, and only now did I reflect on the ambiguity in the term "Them." "They" might well have been the people who had blown up my home.

But then the lights came on, and I could see why they had been turned off: the interior of the vehicle was virtually an electronics laboratory, the walls of which were covered with dials and switches and meters, and cables crisscrossed the floor. A dour man in a spotless coverall and wearing a headset shared this constricted space with the "derelict" and me.

I asked a necessary question: "Who *are* you fellows?"

My bum—who incidentally even in close-up seemed to have genuinely bad skin and bleary eyes, unless it was a masterpiece of makeup—said: "I think you know that sort of thing is never spelled out, really as a matter of taste or style, not because of any need for great secrecy. After all, everybody knows that when some agency goes unnamed, it must be what you think it is and not the Department of Agriculture."

I must say I was relieved. "Ah, you're the—"

"Firm," he said quickly. "Or sometimes the Bunch, or even the Troop. Less often the Pack, but sometimes, jocularly, the Gang. And then—"

The man in the headset broke in querulously: "I'm late for my break, Rasmussen!"

"All right, so go already," Rasmussen replied, in the idiom everyone, even secret agents, picks up when in New York. He took the earphones from the other man and put them across his own crown. He then sat down on a little stool before a panel that was an electronics extravaganza, and switched off the interior lights while the other man slipped out the rear of the van.

When the lights came on again Rasmussen said: "Now then, let's have your story."

"If you'll tell me why you are wearing the headset."

He cocked an eye at me. "I must warn you, Wren: there's no tit for tat in covert work."

"You know my name?"

He looked as though he might have blushed, had his complexion not already been too variegated to show more color. "All right, call me guilty of an indiscretion. I suppose you'd find out anyway, soon enough. We live in a time when it is unfashionable to keep secrets: this is especially true of undercover operatives. Wilcox, there, who just went out for coffee and Danish: I happen to know he sells everything he hears in this job to Sylvester Swan, the muckraking columnist."

"That's neither here nor there," said I. "I demand, under the Freedom of Information Act, to hear what you know about how I was bombed out of house and home this evening, and who that really was who called me and identified himself as the Sebastiani Liberation Front, and how I narrowly escaped before the building blew up, and why the cops and TV people dismissed my efforts to tell them what happened."

Rasmussen was looking at me with a sly smile. "Wren, my dear fellow, you've lots to learn. I suppose you don't realize that you have just fecklessly spilled all the beans in your possession. You have withheld nothing with which to bargain. Suppose you were in the enemy's hands at the moment? Your goose would be well done!"

"Come on, Rasmussen, I'm not playing a game."

"But *we* are, old boy, as you would know if you read any blockbusting thrillers. We're having the time of your lives, and— Wait a minute!" He adjusted the earphones and fiddled with some knobs. His smile became a grin that grew dirtier. "This is rich," he whispered. "His boyfriend just came back from the ballet, three hours late. They're in bed now and having quite a set-to. Somebody's going to burst into tears in a moment, and somebody's going to have to atone."

I winced. "Is it really useful to do that sort of eavesdropping, Rasmussen? So some Russian diplomat is an invert: is that really scandalous nowadays?"

"Russian?" he jeered. "This is ———." The name he gave, which of course I suppress here, was that of a leading American statesman.

"Good gravy, that's worse! How can you possibly justify that sort of thing as legitimate information-gathering?"

Rasmussen scowled. "Don't get pious on me, Wren. Do you want your country to be run like a queer bathhouse?" But his face soon returned to a prurient smirk, in response to what he was hearing. "I can't wait to see the videotapes."

"You've got a hidden TV camera in there?"

"Over the bed," he gloated. "In a phony air-conditioning vent. And of course it's *our* boy in there with that old queen."

"Is there no limit to your swinishness?" I asked in disbelief. "I don't know that I even approved of the Abscam entrapments, and they played only on the natural greed of all men. But sex!"

He stared suspiciously at me. "You're clean in that area, I hope."

"I certainly am! But what's that got to do with—"

"Wren," Rasmussen said, taking off the headset, "sit down here." He gestured at a nearby floorbound coil of cable. I did as he suggested, having nowhere better to go.

He found a pipe somewhere and filled it from a pouch. He lighted up deliberately. "We've had an eye on you for a while," he said at last, spewing some smoke down at me. "You'll be pleased to know you passed every test."

"Test?"

He smiled in that superior, benevolent fashion of the man who has done something disagreeable to you for your own good—doctor, schoolmaster, policeman. "It won't do any harm at this juncture to reveal that Ben Rothman works for us."

"In his deli? By selling pastrami and corned beef?"

Rasmussen took the pipe from his lips and exhaled in a torrent of thick smoke. "And the man who gave you a dollar, outside the French restaurant."

"Oh, come on, what was the purpose of that?"

"Take a look at the bill."

I fished it from my pocket, where it had lain doggo during the attack of the small girls. I uncrumpled and examined the face of the dollar, expecting to find George Washington replaced by the head of a rhesus monkey or the like, but not so.

"Turn it over," said Rasmussen, directing more smoke my way. "Look at the reverse of The Great Seal."

This is the circle to the left, in which is depicted a truncated pyramid surmounted by an eye inside a triangle over which, on a proper bill, is arched the Latin phrase *Annuit Coeptis.* Below the pyramid, on a curved scroll, should properly be *Novus Ordo Seclorum.* On the one I held, the words *Omne Animal* hung over the pyramid, while underneath one could read: *Post Coitum Triste.*

"Very funny," I said sullenly. "All right, you've proved you can make contact with me so delicately that not even I know it. But what's your purpose?"

While I was off guard he snatched the dollar from me, claiming it as the property of the Firm. Sucking on his pipe, which gurgled repulsively, he buried the bill in his pocket. He resumed. "At the moment of greatest emergency, namely when the bomb was about to go off, you not only saved yourself but had the presence of mind to carry that little hooker out of danger."

"Don't tell me Bobbie was still another of your people?"

He shook his head, emitting smoke. " 'Fraid not. She's just a whore so far as we know—unless she works for the Competition. I hope not, because on occasion I've used her services, and

I'd hate to think that in the violent transports of lust I might have disclosed some information from classified material."

"I take it I will eventually hear an explanation of why you posed these challenges to me. Frankly, it had better be plausible."

The rear of the van, which was sealed off from the front seat by a solid partition, was filling with smoke, though seated on the floor as I was, I was still below the worst of it.

Rasmussen asked, "What do you know about Saint Sebastian?"

"Was not the person of that name, if indeed he existed at all, so pierced with the arrows of his enemies that he subsequently became the patron saint of pinmakers?"

Rasmussen scowled. "The Saint Sebastian to which I refer is the little country of that name—"

"Ah! The Sebastiani Liberation Front!"

He closed his eyes in chagrin. "I'm afraid this will get nowhere if you interrupt continually."

"But that's what the voice said on the phone. The only reason I was able to escape the building before it blew up was a call I got about a minute before the explosion: a man with a heavy accent, Slavic perhaps, but with also a bit of the German and God knows what else. On the other hand, I suppose it could have been faked." I peered sharply at Rasmussen: he or one of his colleagues would certainly have been capable of it.

"No news to us," he said disdainfully. "Naturally we had your place wired. That call was made by a member of an underground movement known as the Liberation Front of Saint Sebastian. These people are in the United States at this moment, on a fund- and sympathy-raising campaign for their cause."

"They have chosen a mightily ingratiating means of doing both," said I, showing my teeth. "How dare they come over here and blow up things and ask for *help!* Don't we have enough homegrown scum to do that sort of thing?"

Rasmussen leaned back and displayed a faint derisive smile. "Aren't we becoming a wee bit stuffy, Wren? Wasn't it our own Tom Jefferson who said the tree of liberty should be watered with the blood of tyrants?"

"But who chooses the tyrants? And how many tyrants are

found in Irish working-class homes, London department stores, Israeli kindergartens, and a highway junction near Nyack, New York? All of these have been the sites of unspeakable outrages by terrorist hyenas in the service of some cause for which perhaps some reasonable argument *might* be made, but to murder strangers in its name?"

Rasmussen shrugged. "It's all in a day's work to a pro, Wren. If I got into a tizzy over every little massacre, I'd never get anything accomplished." He grasped the bowl of the pipe and gestured at me with the stem. "Let me fill you in on Saint Sebastian. It's a little principality, tucked away in a kind of side pocket between Austria, Germany, and Czechoslovakia."

"I've *never* heard of a little country in the place you describe. There's Liechtenstein, of course, but isn't that near Switzerland? And San Marino's in Italy—"

"Shut *up*, Wren!" Rasmussen said coarsely. "In covert work we speak only when we have information to impart, never to be sociable."

He used the mispronunciation "coh-VERT," habitual with government types, but I decided to let that go for the moment.

He proceeded, "The place is ruled by one Prince Sebastian the Twenty-third, an anachronism, a dinosaur, an absolutist of the kind you don't nowadays find nowhere, nohow." He had turned folksy without warning: perhaps there are people who find that charming. "He has got away with it probably only because who cares about a tiny state of maybe seventy square miles, say thirty thousand souls, no raw materials of a strategic sort, and furthermore not on the main route to anyplace anybody would want to go, enclosed by high mountains. I mean, this is a little place time forgot, buddy-boy."

While wincing at his meaningless familiarity, I reflected that the same phrase had been uttered by me, on occasion, with reference to my hometown, a dreamy upstream Hudson hamlet where no doubt still today the village officials wear their pants an inch too short.

Rasmussen went on, after having sent my way a burst of smoke so noxious it might have come from the tailpipe of a city bus, "This prince is supposed to be some kind of nut, according to the few informants we have been able to find, a handful of tourists who have visited Saint Sebastian, and an old newsman, a stringer for some wire service, named Clyde McCoy. McCoy has apparently stayed there for years, due to the low cost of living and his high capacity for alcohol, cheap in Saint S. He's not exactly a trench-coated swashbuckler, I gather, not to mention that there's never been much that could be called noteworthy news from the place."

"*I* certainly have never heard of it," I iterated, though well aware that I would be annoying Rasmussen in so doing.

He glared at me briefly, pulling his lips back slightly from the pipe, to display two rows of rather spiky teeth: he was probably of that breed who eventually gnaw a hole in the hard-rubber stem. I seem to part with the rest of the human race in my instinctive distrust of a pipesmoker. "But then, how much do we hear of San Marino and Andorra?" he asked the ceiling of the van—in which incidentally I could spot no much-needed air vent. "Then these bombings began suddenly, as of last month, in certain American cities. I refer to those for which credit has been claimed by the Sebastiani Liberation Front, and not those others that have been the self-proclaimed work of the various other terrorist groups, though one or two explosions are in doubt, being boasted of by two organizations who have apparently no connection with each other, for example, when a series of small charges blew the genitalia off the nude male statuary in the National Gallery, credit was publicly taken by both the Amazon Army, whose cause should be obvious, and the Testosterone Society, an aggregation of militant macho men who performed the mutilation of marble, they said, to highlight society's daily severing of real gonads."

Rasmussen had the execrable taste to grin at this point: I suspected that the last example was apocryphal, his feeble essay at wit. I snorted, and he resumed.

"You can pooh-pooh terrorism in the interests of some schoolboy slogan about the perfectibility of man, but the fact is that violence is just about the only thing that will make you sit up and take notice. We're all in pretty much of a coma nowadays, wouldn't you say, what with mainlining, speedballing, herpes lesions, fear of getting AIDS from a handshake with a kid brother, dioxin-contaminated barbecue pits, over-the-counter medicaments dosed with poison by embittered loners." He produced an anguished gasp: apparently he took modern life as hard as any of us. "Hell, man, it *takes* an explosion to cut through all that shit!"

I wondered again, as I had in the past, whether we were getting the finest types of men for our government bureaus or whether they were going instead into the much more lucrative field of pornographic videocassettes.

"Rasmussen," I asked, "would you mind opening a door or turning on a fan?" I coughed and beat my hands. "Your pipe is asphyxiating."

"Aha," said he, "you reveal a weakness."

"Yes. I'm afraid I breathe air."

He sighed and propped his pipe against a panel of switches and dials. "My point is, if the Sebastiani Liberation group thinks it worth their while to come all the way over here and blow up a dump like the late building in which you made your squalid home, perhaps we should return the favor and examine what it is they are protesting against. Then we might throw our weight to whichever side looks as though it's going to win, instead of getting entangled in ideologies, which is always a sucker's game. What I say is, let's take a look at this bozo close up, this Prince Sebastian. What makes him tick? Maybe if Sebastian comes up clean, it'll bring back the divine right of kings. World could use a new angle on the whole political ball of wax: a rerun of old-fashioned benevolent despotism might be the answer we're all looking for. On the other hand, maybe it will make more sense to fund this Liberation bunch, which might favorably impress various oil-rich fanatics in the Middle East." Rasmussen snatched up his pipe and puffed rapidly. "Well, Wren," he said around the stem, "you'll have a chance to pursue the answer to these questions."

"Me?"

"We've decided to send you there," said he. "Isn't snooping your profession? Obviously if you've survived in New York City you know how to lie and cheat and dissemble: spying should be just your meat."

I chewed on this remarkable proposal for a moment, then said, "Don't think I'm not flattered by your offer, Rasmussen, but really, I can't leave town at the moment. I've got to find a new home, and then I have to reconstruct my play. It's true that I have had some experience as an investigator, but that's pretty remote from being a spy, if you think about it. A principal difference is that if you do a bad job of private detection, it is not routine to be executed."

He failed to acknowledge these sentiments. "Your cover will be this: you're an American playwright who's gone to Saint Sebastian because it's a nice quiet place to hole up and lick your second-act problems."

I must say his information was uncannily accurate in assessing my dramaturgical difficulties. How he could have known about them was beyond me. Had I talked aloud in my sleep in the bugged room?

"Well, if you put it that way, I'll think it over." The fact was that with the winding up of the Rothman Deli job I had no employment. Indeed it would not have been easy to name a time when I had ever been overwhelmed with work. "I don't want to be vulgar," I said, "but am I naïve in assuming you folks pay some kind of fee to the free-lance?"

Rasmussen rose suddenly from his camp chair and hurled himself at the rear doors. I tried to follow him, but he opened the right-hand panel, leaped out, and slammed it in my face: furthermore, locked it from outside. After pounding awhile impotently, I went to assault the windowless metal wall that separated the rear compartment from the cab. The engine roared into life and started to move with a vicious lurch. I fell backwards, striking something adamantine with my head.

2

I WAS SHAKEN awake as the vehicle hit a procession of the profound potholes with which Manhattan streets are pockmarked . . . except that I was not in the van or on a street anywhere, but rather in an airplane, aloft, and the bumps were caused by faults in the sky!

It was a commercial craft, and the approaching stewardess was a substantial fairhaired girl who wore a short dress of green jersey. She brought me a little tray which held a cup of café au lait and a plump croissant.

"Goot morning," said she. "Wilcom to Sebastiani Royal Airline, Meester Wren!" The bosom of her dress yawned open as she bent with the tray. I stared into her luxurious cleavage as something to do while I collected my wits. She asked, "Vould you like to skveese the breasts?" I should say her smile was more genial than sensual.

"Uh, no, thank you," said I, and then, courtesy being my foible even when far from home, I saw fit to add, "Perhaps another time. They look very nice."

"Oh yes," she said with vigor. "Mine body is beautifool." It would be hard to explain that this statement did not sound like boasting when it was pronounced. My natural taste in females is for a more slender sort of blond, but I must say that this statuesque person put me at ease, or at any rate at a good deal more of it than I could have claimed in her absence.

"Miss, please don't think me mad if I ask where we are, where *I* am. Did you say 'Sebastiani'? Is that what it would seem, a reference to the little principality of Saint Sebastian?"

She smiled grandly with the largest of white teeth and an

expanse of rosy lips: she was a spectacularly healthy specimen. "Ve vill be landing there soon."

I took a sip of the coffee, which proved hot and delicious and thus reassuring. "You may not believe this, but I haven't any idea of how I got here. When I was last awake, I was in a vehicle on a street in New York City."

She nodded sympathetically. "You had had some drinks before your friends brought you aboard, I think. You vent to sleep and only now have you awakened up. Vot puzzles me, sir, is how you have retained your you-reen all the night long."

"Pardon me . . . . ?"

She frowned. "Don't you have to make peepee?"

I wasn't prepared for her frankness, which I began to suspect was habitual. I shook my head. I had had nothing to drink since the cheap plonk of my wretched supper: it seemed clear enough that that swine Rasmussen had drugged me. I would be mighty indignant when this flight touched down. Meanwhile there was nothing to do but eat breakfast. Both the coffee and croissant were excellent.

The stewardess said her name was Olga. She seemed to be working alone.

I asked whether there were any other passengers.

"Now, no. Your friends left in Vienna."

"Did one of them have a bad complexion?"

"To be sure," said Olga. She vivaciously sat down in the aisle seat. Her skirt was so short that her columnar thighs were now altogether bare. "I did not like him, forgive me!"

"Neither do I," I freely admitted.

She lifted the hinged seat-arm between us, leaned against me, and peered into my face. Her eyes were very blue. "Foreigners sometimes do not understand our vays. Ve do not have to screw under *every* circumstance. For example, rudeness is a reason not; opening the trousers first, or foul language, or violent seizings! All of these your friend did, forgive me."

"Let me apologize for him," said I. "He's not, thank heavens, typical of my countrymen." I felt some security in expressing this patriotic sentiment. "The average Yank, whom perhaps you haven't been fortunate enough to meet, is a hardworking family man whose simple idea of pleasure is to burn meat on a charcoal grill. He is definitely not a cryptofascist religious-fanatic warmonger, though he is, at work, no Nipponese zealot. He may even be something of a slacker, speaking industrially, but—"

"*You* can screw with me, to be sure," said Olga. She grasped the hem of her perfunctory skirt and raised it, lifting her bottom. She seemed to be wearing no underthings.

I have seldom been found lacking in carnal appetite, but no element in this state of affairs was propitious.

"I'll tell you," I told her, somehow sensing that it would not be considered a rejection, "I'd prefer, right now, to drink another cup of coffee and eat a second croissant."

I was right: she popped up, her skirt falling after a long and not at all unattractive moment, and smiling sweetly as ever, went to do my bidding. This time the croissant was accompanied by a fluffy pale mound, not a poisonously golden pat, of sweet butter and a little Limoges pot of an extraordinarily fragrant honey. Having delivered these, Olga sat down next to me again. She, too, exuded a lovely bouquet similar to that of the honey. I mentioned it to her, and she told me that both honey and scent traced their origins to a wild flower peculiar to the high meadows of her country. I must say that the associations the name Saint Sebastian had today were preferable to those of the evening before.

I could not forgive Rasmussen for the manner in which he had shanghaied me, but while finishing my breakfast I did remember the job for which I had been hired.

"Tell me, Olga," I said, gesturing with half a croissant, "about your prince."

"What is to be told?"

I nibbled and swallowed. "Is he loved by the people of Saint Sebastian?"

"Why nawt?" She laughed *hahaha*.

"Umm. But you know what I mean: is he *really* liked, admired, and so on, or does he simply hold power by brute force?"

"Ah," she sighed. "I could never know about that. My job is to be stewardess, and not to deal in social theoretics, you see."

It occurred to me to ask, "Do you even have the vote?"

"No, indeed, God be thanked!" Her negative enthusiasm seemed genuine enough.

I swallowed the remainder of the buttered and honeyed croissant and finished the coffee. They seemed to have a soporific effect. I barely had the energy to put another question.

"You are aware, are you not, of an anti-Prince Opposition? In fact, a terrorist group that blows up buildings in New York to get attention for its cause? The Sebastiani Liberation Front?"

Olga smiled prettily at me throughout my questions, in that fashion in which the questioned seems amused by some ad hominem reflections on the questioner and gives little heed to what is being asked. I wondered whether she was a nymphomaniac or merely weak-minded: I had known both sorts, sometimes even in combination, but never had they been so magnificently salubrious. I confess that Olga had an odd effect on me at this point: I would rather have trained her for some sporting event than taken her to bed.

I waved my hand before her eyes. "Did you hear me?"

She filled her great bosom with air and released it in a happy kind of gasp. "I am too beautiful for such matters. I vas selected for the job I have now soon after my breasts began to grow."

The gentle gong-sound that accompanies the seat-belt sign was heard, and Olga informed me that the airplane was about to land. She went to the little fold-down perch beside the door to the cockpit, giving me another vista of her breathtaking thighs. I reluctantly turned from this spectacle to the view from the window. I saw some neat checkerboarded farmland below, in various shades of earth colors, and then soon enough we were over clustered dwellingplaces, crooked streets, and free-form shapes of greenery, several of which surrounded bodies of water that reflected the cerulean sky, and on a higher elevation what seemed to be a crenellated stone fortress, and then the airplane made a great sweeping, banking turn and smoothly descended onto a very simple blacktopped landing strip, coming to rest nowhere near the terminal building, which in any event was too small to be equipped with an extensible gangway.

Olga opened the door, and I went to join her. To see outside, I had to lean around this magnificent specimen of young-womanhood, who was at least as tall as I. Beyond the airfield in that direction the farmland began, and in the distance I saw a blue range of mountains. I knew no more of the geography of this part of the world than I knew of its language, politics, history, or culture. Why Rasmussen felt it necessary to hustle me off so quickly, with no preparation or opportunity for research, made no sense, unless it could be explained by calling him a bureaucratic scoundrel and having done with it.

At this point a fairhaired functionary on the ground outside began to maneuver a portable stairway into place at the door of the aircraft.

"Good-bye, sir," said Olga. "I hope you did enjoy the flight anyway."

"Good-bye, Olga. You're a nice girl." On an impulse I added, "I regret not being in the mood to screw this morning. Perhaps another time."

"When you want!" she answered ebulliently, performing a little curtsy.

I went down the metal stairs and stepped onto the tarmac. The man who had wheeled the stairway into place was gone. Olga was still the only person I had seen since the night before, and no one was in sight on the airfield. The terminal building was a good half mile away from where I stood. Just as I decided that I would have to hike for it, I heard the distant racket of a noisy engine, and a vehicle came onto the field and rapidly approached me. When it got nearer I recognized it as an ancient station wagon of American make, a vintage model with a body of real wooden panels. It had been indifferently maintained: black smoke gushed from its tailpipe, and much of the wooden paneling was in a sorry condition, rotting or splintered. The windshield was cracked, the tires were bald, the front bumper was loose at one end. Instead of glass, plastic sheeting covered the driver's window. This was so dirty and discolored that I could not identify the person at the wheel until he stopped the car and cried out in a voice that seemed to come from the throat of a man with a mortal illness.

"You Wren?"

I could not see the speaker, but I confirmed the identification.

"Climb aboard!" The passenger's door was flung open. When I had rounded the old station wagon at the rear—the windows of which had been glazed with water-stained cardboard—I saw that the door had been opened so violently, and had been so feebly hinged, that in fact it lay on the runway.

I leaned down and looked in at the driver.

He fell across the seat in my direction, hand outthrust in greeting. "Clyde McCoy. Good to see somebody from Home."

Of course, he was the man Rasmussen had mentioned.

I thrust my hand in and shook his. "What should I do about the door?"

McCoy managed to sit up. He was a skinny, sinewy individual and dressed in a dark-gray suit that I suspected to be properly light gray. His urine-yellow shirt had surely begun life as white. The hue of his tie could be called grease-green. He left the car and staggered around the hood to reach the fallen door. He was one of those persons who owing to slightness of figure and lifelessness of hair could be any age. Using what seemed the strength of sudden madness, he lifted the door and got it back on its hinges. He closed it gingerly. Then he reached through the glassless aperture, found a twisted coat hanger that hung there, and fastened the wire to the upright post of the frame. This took a few moments of intense application in which he breathed in upon me, and when the job was done I felt half drunk.

When he returned to fit himself in back of the wheel I asked apprehensively, "You wouldn't want me to drive?"

He peered at me through lids that were almost closed. "It's understandable you think I'm under the influence. I suffer from a disease that resembles drunkenness so closely that my breath even seems to smell of alcohol. That's why I first came to this country. Saint Sebastian had the only doctor in the world at the time who knew how to treat this ailment. You know what he prescribed? Schnapps. Lots of it. You'd notice if I were to take a drink or two now I'd be sober in no time."

The vehicle was so old that its starter was mounted on the floor, and after making his statement McCoy began to look for it with the toe of his right foot, which was shod in a battered old shoe from which a section had been cut out, presumably to favor a bunion.

"I suppose you know that Rasmussen sent me," I said. "But what you might not know is that I've had no preparation for the assignment. I don't even have any money or a passport. And what language is spoken here? I want to get hold of a dictionary or phrase book."

"Don't worry about anything," McCoy answered. "I'll be back to normal in no time." He had begun to shake, but he finally got the starter's range and brought the engine into deafening life. The car jerked into motion and sped towards the terminal building.

It occurred to me to ask: "Don't I have to go through Immigration and/or Customs?"

The question fortunately came just in time to halt McCoy's head in its descent to the steering wheel. He lifted it and said, "Naw."

If we had continued on the current course we would have driven directly through the little terminal building. I urged McCoy to turn, which he did abruptly, lifting us on two wheels.

"But," I pointed out when the car had regained its equilibrium and left the airport on what was presumably the exit road, an unpaved, rutted lane, "am I not making an illegal entry?" I turned to see whether we would be pursued, but could not, owing to the cardboard in the back window.

McCoy frowned. Looking at me, he forgot the road. I leaned over and seized the rim of the wheel with both hands and kept it steady.

I was worried. "Hadn't we better switch places?"

McCoy shook himself and reclaimed the wheel. "I'm fine. I just need a little pick-me-up and I'll even be better."

We were entering a town, shaking along a narrow cobblestoned street that wound past clustered stone buildings, going over an occasional bridge, also of stone. We passed through more than one quaint square around which were a bakery, a cafe, an *épicerie*, and sometimes a spired church. But human beings were not to be seen.

Finally McCoy pulled against a high curb, scraping, with an awful sound, not only the tires but the edges of the wheels as well.

"Got to stop this way," said he. "The brakes are pretty far gone, and except in the royal garages mechanics are in short supply. Except for foreigners, and of course the prince, cars aren't permitted in Saint Sebastian. Better slide out this way, so I don't have to undo that door again." He left the vehicle.

I slid over and out and stepped onto the stones of the next street I had touched after leaving the asphalt of Third Avenue, New York City. We were before a modest five- or six-story structure labeled, over its plain entrance, Hotel Bristol.

Once on his feet, McCoy magically gained a certain sobriety and positively loped into the hotel. I followed, entering a small lobby furnished with a high desk behind which were a set of birdhouse mailboxes and a panel from which hung outsized keys of dull brass. This complex was controlled by a stout person with a handlebar mustache. He wore an ancient-looking tailcoat, which I suspect would on closer examination have proved all but threadbare. His wing collar was none too clean, and the posy in his lapel was browning. He gave me a quick frown and then a slow, broad smile that eventually reached the gold tooth on the far left.

"Sir, without doubt you are Mr. Wren." He spun around, frighteningly fast for a fat man, and seized one of the hanging keys. He placed the key on the counter and rang the little domed bell there. From nowhere came a teenaged boy in a green monkey suit with brass buttons. He saluted me with two fingers and was about to pick up the key when, remembering I had no money in my pockets, I shook my head. Call me a tender soul, but I cannot stand to stiff a servitor.

"No, no," I said. "I'll find it myself. I have no luggage."

The concierge leaned onto his desk and, lowering his heavy head, winked ponderously. "He is available for more than carrying bags, sir."

For an instant I did not get his drift, being impatient to follow McCoy, who, oblivious to me, was already opening the grillwork door of the tiniest elevator I had ever seen.

"Then," my oily questioner persisted, "shall I send up a person of the remaining sex?"

"Neither," I blurted, and as he was beginning a response that I feared might well extend to zoological matters, I snatched up the key and stepped towards the lift. But I was too late. The feckless McCoy was already ascending in the little cage, his runover shoes just at the level of my nose, through the brass grille of the door.

It took an eternity for the elevator to return, throughout which I had an unpleasant wait, for the concierge renewed his importunities in a crooning, obsequious voice that was more repulsive than what he was suggesting.

The lift finally returned, and I took it to the fourth floor, being directed there by the number on the key. When I found my room, the door was open and there, before a rickety desk-table, stood McCoy, draining into his mouth the last few drops from an upended flat pint vessel. His lower lip was dippered out like that of a performing chimpanzee who has learned to drink Coke from the bottle.

He saw me when he lowered the now dead soldier. "All right," he said bitterly, "so I have a little snort now and again, so send me before the firing squad. Other people kill, torture, mutilate, yet never hear a word of criticism, but let me just take a little drink and I'm a criminal." He bent in the ever so careful movement of the drunk and deposited the empty bottle in a little wastecan under the desk. Then he went to an opened suitcase that lay on the bed and began to root through the clothing therein. "Rats," he gasped, growing more desperate and eventually hurling the valise's contents onto the coverlet. "Did you bring only one bottle?"

"I wasn't even permitted to bring a change of clothing," I told him indignantly, remembering my plight. "I assume I can get outfitted on one your local accounts."

"This is your luggage," he said in disgust. "It beat us here from the airport."

"Mine?" Except what I was wearing, tan corduroys and a knitted shirt in dark green, my own wardrobe, such as it had been, had perished in the explosion in New York. That Rasmussen had had time to collect the contents of this valise suggested that he had prepared for my mission far in advance of my being informed of it. The realization did nothing for my souring mood.

"Kindly get away from my possessions," I told McCoy. "I gather you have just drained the bottle the Firm included for my own medicinal uses."

McCoy sank to a seat on the edge of the bed. "If I don't get another drink I'm going to die."

And he had only just finished a pint of ardent spirits!

"What you need, my friend," I told him, "is rather a thorough drying out. I don't know whether Saint Sebastian has a chapter of the good AA folk, but you must take all possible measures towards eventual teetotalling. I'm no bluenose when it comes to drink, but—"

He had begun to shake violently. "You f-f-fucking idiot," he murmured. "I'm dying." With one great hug of his midsection he hurled himself onto the carpet, writhed fiercely, then went still and silent. I was relieved to see he had passed out: I should have been ill put to deal with delirium tremens.

I looked through the clothes provided for me. Alas, Rasmussen's taste, if he had selected them, was deplorable. The jacket was of that madras which is altogether innocent of India, in an awful blue-and-red plaid that has no reference to Scotland. The polyester trousers celebrated the principal bad-taste colors, kelly green, turquoise, and magenta. The loafers were of artificial leather and adorned with tassels. I had not traveled in some years, but I wondered whether the Firm's idea of typical American tourist attire was up to the minute in an age when quiche and *pasta primavera* had become popular even in the hinterlands.

I looked down at McCoy. Could he be genuinely ill? For the first time I actually thought about his having, good God, chug-a-lugged a pint of whiskey in the time it took me to rise on the elevator! I retrieved the empty bottle from the wastecan.

The label identified its late contents as having been no brand of potable spirits but rather an after-shave lotion cutely packaged to resemble a pint of Scotch. I sniffed at its neck: the odor was certainly lethal.

I knelt and searched for a pulse at various places on McCoy's body. I could not find one, nor could I find a house phone when I rose, and when I dashed down the hall to the elevator, there was no response to the finger I pressed repeatedly against the button.

I found a stairway behind an unmarked door at the end of the corridor and hurled myself down it, two steps per vault. Having miraculously reached the bottom without breaking a bone, I burst into the lobby.

The corpulent functionary behind the desk leered at me. "Aha, I knew you would change your mind and want the boy after all!"

"Quick," I cried, "a doctor! Mr. McCoy has been poisoned."

"That is not possible. He only just went to his room."

"Don't argue with me! He's dying of poison, I say. Call a doctor!"

The concierge reached under his counter and brought up one of those ornate brass vintage telephones, reproductions of which are now sold in American discount stores. He barked into the mouthpiece, "Constabulary!" When the connection had been made, he said, "Hotel Bristol. One tourist has poisoned another. . . . Yes." Having put away the telephone, he found an automatic pistol in the desk, brought it up, and trained it on me.

I raised my hands, but protested vigorously. "I'm no killer, and for God's sake will you call an ambulance!"

The concierge rolled his eyes, and his upper lip came down. "Our hotel is not a refuge for gangsters." From his left hand he extended the index finger and waved it before my nose.

The police arrived promptly, two of them, on bicycles, which they trundled into the lobby. These lawmen were uniformed as if for an operetta: braided tunics, high glossy boots, caps like pots, and very small holstered pistols. They carried truncheons. The one in the lead had porcine nostrils and was about my height but much wider. Without a word he produced a pair of what proved to be handcuffs and attached ankle manacles, linked by a chain so short that when the other constable had knelt and fettered me with the lower shackles after the first had braceleted my wrists, I was necessarily a hunchback.

I was bent (though not in the British sense), but not mute. "You can't do this to an American national," I blustered, hoping that they would not throw recent Iranian events in my face. "I demand to see my consul."

The larger policeman struck me deftly on the crazybone of my right arm, which was thereby paralyzed for many minutes. "You have no passport," he said after a perfunctory search of my person. "You have no other papers and no money. You are a stateless vagrant, and you are a murderer. On the first charge you are sentenced to a flogging. On the second, to probable death: it would be unkind to predict another outcome to the Hunt."

I had to slow down the centrifuge inside my head, and choose which point to make first. "I'm not a murderer, for heaven's sake. *Flogging?* Probable *death?*" Already my neck was aching from trying to look up at him. "What's the Hunt?"

The smaller constable spoke for the first time. He had a soft, round, bespectacled face and looked like a village schoolteacher, but so had Heinrich Himmler.

"You will not find here the brutality of other countries," said he. "We do not sentence murderers to prison terms, and we do not perform so-called executions. We have the Hunt. We provide the condemned homicide with a revolver."

I was crippled by an utter lack of belief that this was happening. "Let's go back to the beginning, I beg of you," I said. "A fellow American, Mr. Clyde McCoy, by accident drank an entire pint of after-shave lotion. I rushed down here to summon a doctor, since there's no phone in the room—"

"The Hunt," said the pigfaced policeman, "consists of your being released with the pistol and our following your trail with the intention of killing you on sight."

"Just a moment, you policemen can only accuse me of a crime. You can't serve as judge and jury too."

Pigface put the end of his truncheon just under my nose and raised it, to give me a hog's snout as well. "Remember, this is Saint Sebastian, not the USA. We believe that only the policeman is capable of making these judgments, for isn't it only he who deals with the criminals and investigates the crime? Where is the judge all this while? In bed with his mistress! And the members of the jury are going about their little bourgeois affairs in safety and comfort. How can any of these people know of criminal matters as well as, not to say better than, the law-enforcement officer? And why should Sebastianers take seriously the so-called rights of those whose profession it is to damage those who observe the law?"

In this debate, if such it was, I was hampered by more or less agreeing with him, after years of residence in New York, where generally speaking the only citizen whose life is without hazard is the ruthless felon. But by the same token, *viz.*, being a New Yorker, I was culturally constrained to bring into use the word "fascist," which is literally meaningless except in a use peculiar to Mussolini, but which in Manhattan is regularly applied to any projected inconvenience.

The Sebastiani cops snorted in indifference, and the smaller said, "So why should we care what name be given the practice? The point is, there are crimes and criminals here as elsewhere, for roguery is natural to mankind, but there are no *habitual* criminals."

"We should surely see eye to eye on this subject," I said, "were *I* not unjustly accused, arrested, and restrained. There's the flaw in your practice!"

"And this is to demonstrate *your* flaw," the shorter policeman replied, and struck me across the kidneys with his truncheon. "You are helpless."

He had made his painful point, and I sensed that it would be politic for me to stay silent, but I could not accept the unfairness of it. "Won't you at least get medical help for my friend McCoy? There might still be hope for him."

"Aha," said the larger man. "You are the sort of pervert whose pleasure is bringing some poor devil to the threshold of death and then reviving him so that you can do it all over again?"

It seemed hopeless, and they were about to conduct me to the police station (by walking me in my bonds between them on their bikes, I assumed), where I would be given the aforementioned pistol and sent out as prey for the Hunt, when the little lift came down to the lobby and who should emerge but McCoy, not good as new, which would probably not have characterized him even as a child, I suspect, but certainly better than when last seen.

He lurched up to my captors and asked, "What are you scumheads doing to my friend? Get him out of those bracelets or I'll drive those billy clubs up your fat rumps."

Both officers blanched, and each contested with the other to be first to comply with the abusive demands.

While with twenty blundering thumbs they undid my various

restraints McCoy asked, "Why did you let them do this to you, Wren?"

"They're armed, for God's sake."

"Why," said he, "that doesn't mean anything. Look." He booted the larger officer in the behind. The victim looked only more miserable. He had hung the strap of his stick over his holster, and he failed to make a move towards either of his weapons.

"But they represent the law," I pointed out.

He gave me his bleary eyes. His breath stank of shaving lotion. "Only if you agree to let them."

"You mean what's legal or not is arguable in Saint Sebastian? That if I actually *had* murdered you I could righteously refuse to be arrested?"

"Murdered me?"

"I thought you were dying after drinking that stuff. I was looking for a doctor."

McCoy snorted. "It's that disease I told you I had. I didn't get the booze down quickly enough, so I passed out. But I came to when the alcohol had had time to take hold. By the way, somebody put the wrong label on that bottle. It's not Scotch but rye, and not a bad one. Decent booze is hard to get here unless you visit the prince. Schnapps is the local firewater."

Could there be such a malady? Perhaps I had misjudged him. But apart from that, he obviously had a stainless-steel gastrointestinal system.

My back ached. I was tempted to take a kick at the policemen myself, but I was still far from certain as to the rules or lack thereof in this situation. It would take me a while to lose my inhibitions against assaulting officers armed with guns and clubs, though that sort of thing was routine enough back home.

But complaining to the manager of the place one is currently living in is always permissible if not obligatory. I stepped up to the obese person back of the desk.

Before I could speak he crooned, "Ah, *now* you want a boy."

I lost such little patience as I had retained. "No, you pederast's ponce! How dare you accuse me of murder and put me through that humiliation?"

He stared at me for a while, I think to determine whether I

was serious, and then he called back the policemen, who were just rolling their bicycles out the door. My heartbeat became irregular. Despite McCoy, were they going to re-arrest me?

But when they reached the desk, the fat man came out from behind his protection and extended his hands.

"It's the pillory for me, I'm afraid. This gentleman charges me with exaggerated rudeness."

The constables assumed stern expressions and proceeded to put him into the arrangement of manacles and chains from which I had only lately been freed. I felt no triumph. Indeed, I tried to register my protest—all I wanted was a simple apology and, more important, to establish the truth that those who make accusations should have sound evidence in support—I was about to ask the policemen to free the concierge, but McCoy restrained me.

"Don't interfere," said he. "That's their way. I never make any trouble except when it's my own ox being gored. Besides, he *should* be punished. That's no way to run a hotel."

The policemen led the fat man away, riding their bikes on either side of him, at none too slow a pace even while still within the hotel, so that he was forced to perform a brisk trot, which was anything but dignified for a man of his bulk.

I said to McCoy, "Those policemen brought their bikes in here? In New York that would make sense, but I thought these people didn't steal."

"You haven't got the right idea yet," said he. "There's some theft here. What's different is that nobody can make a career of it, if he loses a hand for every conviction."

I took an extra breath. I had heard that that punishment, for which Xenophon had praised the younger Cyrus, was still being exacted in remote regions of Arabia, but in mid-Europe in the late twentieth century? This was turning out to be an appalling little principality.

"But are there still Sebastianers who would risk the loss of a hand for a bicycle, furthermore a bicycle that could easily be traced in so small an area and population?"

"It can't be news to you that human beings do things at which they can be hurt," McCoy said, with an appropriately cynical turn at one corner of his mouth. "Maybe *because* they'll get hurt." He frowned. "I wonder whether I need a drink to hold me until we get to the palace."

"Palace?"

"Uh-huh," he replied negligently. "The prince has invited us to lunch."

"The sovereign of Saint Sebastian? This is incredible."

"Don't make too much of it," McCoy said sourly. "Not that many tourists come here, the foreign diplomats left years ago, and he is afraid he might get assassinated if he sees his subjects, so he gets lonely." He started for the door. There was no one at the hotel desk now that the concierge had been arrested, but that was not my problem.

We got into the car and McCoy drove, inordinately as ever, down the cobblestoned street, all but grazing a skirted priest wearing a wide-brimmed hat and riding a shabby bicycle. In response the man of peace raised a warlike fist. He was thus far the only person I had seen at large.

Soon we entered upon a steep ascent that would have been an effort for a powerful new vehicle. At times the soles of my feet were seemingly higher than my chin, and the ancient car had a deeper cough and a more violent shudder for each yard of the road. But we finally reached the summit and rolled across a paved area large enough to be a parade ground and approached the palace, which without doubt was the castlelike structure I had seen from the air. It was massive and of a chunky stone texture, with narrow slits for windows and a roofline of crenellations, really more of a fortress than a palace, if one thinks ideally of the latter as being characterized first by stateliness.

Sebastian's robust residence suggested it could hold off an army—not one armed with nuclear weapons, certainly, or perhaps even howitzers, but certainly swords, maces, and battleaxes, and maybe even flintlocks, would be no threat to anyone within its walls.

We arrived before a great entrance gate, but could not use it until its massive door was lowered over the moat, which, probably because I had been staring up, I had not noticed before. McCoy stopped the car by colliding with an abutment. He blew the horn, and hard upon the echo the enormous door, made of thick wood bound and studded with iron, began its creaking descent. I was disappointed, when it was altogether down, not to be able to see into a courtyard, for another large door intruded.

We crossed the drawbridge, found a winding staircase in the tower to the left, and climbed, emerging eventually into a windowless room. As yet we had heard or seen no living thing, but now two men, in even more gaudy operetta uniforms than the police had worn, entered through one of the several doors in the far wall. They were husky young officers with ruddy cheeks; except for their eyes (respectively ferret and hound) and noses (Roman and snub), they might have been twins.

"Good day, Mr. McCoy," said the one in the lead. "Perhaps you have explained the procedure to Mr. Wren."

"More or less," said my companion. He turned to me. "They search you, and then you put on the kimono."

The second officer assigned himself to me. He was the one with the beady bright eyes and large nose. "How do you do," said he, clicking his heels. "Mr. Wren. I am Lieutenant Blok. Please to come along to the changing room, if you will."

He led me to one of the doors. McCoy, lurching along behind the other officer, gave me a smirk. The changing room was a small chamber furnished with a chair and a plain table that held what looked like a stack of navy-blue towels.

I stood there and did nothing for a while, not knowing quite what the drill was, and not wanting to be notably quick in stripping myself before a man.

As if reading me, Blok after a moment asked politely, "Would you prefer a female guard?"

Funny, but this offer did not seem as flattering to my sense of my own virility as it might have. "Certainly not," I replied, and in no time at all was down to my briefs—the rather gaudily striped pair I had purchased, for a song, from a sidewalk vendor's cardboard box on Fourteenth Street: how could I have known, upon donning them two mornings ago, that they would not be doffed until I was in a castle in a foreign land, about to meet an absolute monarch?

As each of my few articles of clothing came off it was handed to Lieutenant Blok, who examined it carefully. He now received my socks, which after two days might well have been a bit high.

"You must understand," I said to this spotless officer in his shining boots, "I was whisked over here—" and then I remembered that as a secret agent I should probably not volunteer such details, though Rasmussen, with the same negligence that had characterized this assignment from the first, had failed to give me any such instructions. "I'm an impulsive traveler," I said. "I jumped on the plane before I had a chance to shower."

Blok made no reply, just continued solemnly to inspect the socks—as if one could conceal a lethal weapon there, despite the sizable hole in each toe.

And I'm sorry to say that I finally had to surrender even the striped drawers for the same search, and then was obliged to bend and spread my nether cheeks, should I be concealing a vial of explosive.

3

WHEN BLOK FINISHED his inspection he bowed and left the room, and immediately in came a little officer resplendent in braid and wearing a sword. He clicked his heels.

"Mr. Wren, I am General Anton Popescu, commander of the Life Guards." He took from the table what turned out to be, when unfolded, a rather handsome ankle-length robe of thick soft stuff, a kind of velour without excessive sheen, in a blue I now would call not quite as dark as navy. I put on this garment with considerable relief, and was next provided with a pair of sandals of soft black calfskin, soled with crepe rubber.

When I was dressed, the little general, who wore the thinnest of mustaches and whose hair was brilliantined and parted in the middle, opened the door through which he had come, bowed, and swept me onward with an expansive gesture. I found myself in a marble-floored corridor, the walls of which were lined with magnificent tapestries.

McCoy was waiting there, wearing a robe like mine. He said sardonically, "I see you weren't carrying a grenade up your keister."

I addressed the general. "These tapestries are splendid."

"Indeed they are," he told me. "When Leo the Tenth heard about them he demanded that Raphael make similar designs for the Vatican."

"Do you mean—"

"To be sure," said Popescu. "And for those the master was paid ten thousand ducats. These he did for the rewards of piety and the gratitude of Sebastian the Fifteenth."

"The history of this country goes back that far?"

"Good gracious," said Popescu, running a finger along one side of his mustache. "This country was venerable by the time of the Renaissance. There were Sebastianers who went on the First Crusade with Walter the Penniless, though to be sure few survived the journey through Bulgaria. They were wont to plunder the lands they passed through, you see, and sometimes the people who lived there took countermeasures. Sebastian the Third himself went to the Fourth Crusade: his Byzantine souvenirs can be found amidst the palace collections."

As I dimly remembered, the Fourth was the farcical crusade: en route to smite the infidels, the Western Europeans stopped off to assault their fellow Christians at Byzantium and sack that great city. But it would scarcely be politic to make this point at that moment. Instead I indicated the nearest tapestry, on which was depicted a kneeling haloed individual about to have his brains bashed out by the boulder held high over the head of the person behind him.

"Who's that poor devil?"

"Saint Stephen, being stoned," said the general. "You know those old martyrs!"

McCoy was either blasé from having seen the tapestries too often or, more likely, had no taste for the fine arts. He was biting his lip and staring longingly down the corridor towards what one would assume was the expected source of his next drink: he had not had one for a good twenty minutes.

We went through a doorway into a large chamber, the walls of which were lined with dark-red silk against which were hung ornately framed oils, all of which were immediately recognizable.

I asked Popescu, "Isn't that a copy of 'Aristotle Contemplating the Bust of Homer'?" The original of which was of course one of the Metropolitan's most publicized possessions.

"In fact," said the little general, wiggling his mustache-lined upper lip, "*this* is the original, done by Rembrandt for his patron Prince Sebastian the Nineteenth. If you have seen another elsewhere in the world, it is surely derivative of this."

"Rembrandt was here?"

"Ah, my friend," sighed Popescu, "he was but one of the many painters to the court of Saint Sebastian."

I stared at the other walls, recognizing Botticelli's "Birth of Venus" and then one of the finest of the many portraits of Philip IV done by the great master whom he kept at the Spanish court.

"Velásquez was one of them?"

"Certainly," said the general, indicating the polished brass plate on the picture frame.

I peered in close-up and read, "Portrait of Sebastian XV, by Diego Rodríguez de Silva y Velásquez, 1599–1660."

"This is remarkable," I disingenuously noted. "Are you aware that this very face, in its many depictions, is elsewhere in the world invariably believed to be that of the Spanish monarch Philip the Fourth?"

The general gestured. "It does not surprise me at all. There have been many such misrepresentations throughout the centuries. No doubt it should be flattering to know that the world so envies us."

I nodded at the "Botticelli" across the room. "Now, that superb canvas is elsewhere called 'Birth of Venus' and sometimes, jocularly, 'Venus on the Half Shell.' " Popescu remained sober. "I believe it is the Uffizi which has an excellent example of it, which, naïfs or prevaricators, they call the original that came from the brush of the sublime Sandro."

The general shrugged with all of his tense little body. "There you are, eh? And don't ever think those wily Florentines naïve, my dear chap! Though it is true enough that Sebastian the Fourteenth more than once made an ass of Lorenzo, who between you and me was not all that Magnificent. . . . As everyone knows, the model for that picture was Queen Sebastiana the Third, done by Botticelli when he was her court painter and perhaps something more." He gave me a significantly cocked eyebrow.

"Remarkable! A nude depiction of a reigning princess?"

General Popescu smiled in pride. "Our rulers have often been notable for their lack of shame."

"They've all been called Sebastian or the female version?"

"No," said Popescu. "There have been Maximilians, Ferdinands, and at least one Igor."

"And surely amongst the princesses' names were Isabella and Carlotta?"

"Indeed," said the general. "I see you've done your homework."

We went through two more rooms hung with the pictorial treasures of the Renaissance. McCoy had long since disappeared.

Finally Popescu said, "Forgive me, but I must take you to the prince. He does not care to wait for his meals!"

He led me to a doorway and stepped aside. I went through it and was met by a horse-faced lackey wearing a green tailcoat, buff knee-breeches, white stockings, and buckled shoes. He held a tall staff, which, as I stepped across the threshold, he lifted and thumped buttfirst upon the floor.

He cried, "Mr. Russel Wren!"

Good gravy, I was in the throne room! There, at the far end of a crimson runner, on a three-stepped stage, sat Prince Sebastian XXIII, or anyway it was to be presumed that the distant figure was he: I would have to walk an eighth of a mile to be certain, between two ranks of trumpeters who, hard on the final echo of the stentorian announcement of my name, raised their golden instruments to their lips and began to sound a deafening fanfare. When these musicians were at last done, my head remained, for almost the entire trip down the carpet, as a cymbal newly struck, and the prince was a growing but tremulous image, so agitated was my vision.

He wore a golden crown and red, ermine-trimmed robe.

As I reached the last ten feet of the red runner, it occurred to me that I must make the traditional gesture of obeisance that was probably expected of everyone, even an American democrat, who finds himself before a throne, but still shaky from the fanfare and utterly unprepared for this moment—wretched Rasmussen, to ship me over without adequate training!—I made a fool of myself: I forgot about bowing, which in fact I had not done since appearing, with powdered hair, in a grammar-school re-enactment of Cornwallis's surrender at Yorktown, and instead plucked an imaginary skirt at either side of mid-thigh while dipping at one knee. In a word, I curtsied.

This performance was greeted with explosive laughter from the throne. "How do you do, Mr. Wren," said the prince, still shaking with mirth. "Welcome to my country."

"Thank you, sir."

His plump face was the kind that one assumed had been almost beautiful as a boy, and he still had rosy cheeks and long-lashed dark eyes. With a hand to steady his crown, he now stood up. He looked to be of medium height. The long red robe concealed the particulars of his body, but there could be no doubt that he was very corpulent.

"Shall we go to lunch," he said, without the implication of a question mark. Lifting the robe slightly, so that the hem would not trip him up, he descended the stairs. When he stood beside me I saw that he was not nearly so tall as I had supposed when viewing him from a lower level: the eminence and the long robe had created an illusion. In reality he was much shorter than I. Which is not, however, to say he lacked that mysterious presence called royal.

A liveried lackey preceded us to the dining room, which was not so far distant from the throne room as I should have supposed, given the size of the palace. The dining room itself was enormous, with a table long enough to have fed dozens. A little army of formally dressed servitors was lined up in silent ranks.

An aged man, festooned with gold chains and keys, shuffled up to meet his sovereign. But what he had to say was reproving. "You shouldn't be wearing that crown. It's not at all the thing to wear at table, it really isn't."

"You old fool," Sebastian said, "it's my crown and I'll wear it when I please. Don't interfere or I'll have you flayed." So much for the words: his delivery, uncertain and even a bit fearful, was at odds with them.

The old man came forward then and, putting out his tremulous hands, took the crown from the prince's head. "Now, you just eat your lunch like a good boy, and we'll say no more about it." He gestured to one of the servingpeople, a young man with large ears, and gave him the crown, which was golden and encrusted with bright gems. It was the first I had ever seen in use, and frankly it did not altogether escape vulgarity: the jewels looked synthetic.

Sebastian made no resistance, but he stamped his foot once his head was bare. "I did so want to wear it for once while eating. You are a withered old person, a feebleminded dotard." His short dark hair showed the impress of the crown.

Immune to the abuse, the old man limped to the head of the table, pulled out the stately chair there, and said, "You just sit down and have your ice cream, young man, and no more nonsense."

I was amazed to see the prince promptly do as told, though he was still muttering peevishly.

He said to me, "I suppose you wonder why I tolerate the insolence of this wretched old thing, but he's been my personal retainer since childhood. There's no one else I can trust, you see."

I had not been told where to sit, and not wanting to call attention to myself—it's strange how the presence of royalty makes bad taste of what would otherwise be routine—I shyly slid out the chair on Sebastian's right and sat down.

The prince picked up a large soup spoon and began to bang it on the tabletop. This sort of infantile demonstration was familiar to me from visits to my married sister, whose daughter, my niece, was an unusually disagreeable baby as well as one of the ugliest children I had ever seen, a dead ringer for my jawless, flap-eared brother-in-law.

"Ice cream!" Sebastian was shouting. "I want my ice cream." These complaints went on for some time, no doubt because Rupert moved so slowly. But at last the old retainer wheeled up to the table a trolley on which, embedded in a tank full of crushed ice, was what would appear to be a canister of vanilla ice cream of the capacity of several gallons. Amidst the chains with which he was hung, Rupert found a golden spoon. He plunged this implement into the container and carefully gathered some ice cream within its bowl. He brought the spoon up but did not taste its contents before inhaling the aroma with quivering nostrils. At last he took the spoon's burden between his desiccated lips, chewed awhile, rheumy eyes rolling, and then brought up from behind him, in his left hand, a shallow silver vessel and, turning away from the prince, but towards me, deliberately spat out the melted residue of what he had been tasting. This was not a palate-piquing spectacle.

The prince cackled maliciously. "I look forward to the day when someone *has* poisoned it, you ancient swine, and you fall to the floor and die, foaming at the mouth and writhing in agony."

Rupert's dried-apple countenance stayed noncommittal as, using two spoons, he built, within a capacious golden bowl, a Himalayan peak of ice cream. Sebastian watched the project with every appearance of mesmerization. When the mountain had at last been sculptured to Rupert's taste, the old man lifted a gold sauceboat high as his shoulder and poured from it a stream of butterscotch syrup onto the summit of the vanilla Everest. From other golden vessels he took, in turn, whipped cream, crushed nuts, chocolate sprinkles, those edible little silver beads, and finally a garishly red maraschino cherry.

When Sebastian saw that the dish had been completed, his importunate cries became more shrill, and when the old retainer at last delivered it to him he fell upon it with a ferocity for which the word "attacked" would be a euphemism. So swift was his work that for an instant I believed he was using no tool but rather shoveling it in with both bare fists. But after my eye adjusted to the motion I could identify, along with the spoon in his right hand, a fork in his left, and though he ate so rapidly, he employed these instruments with the deftness of a surgeon.

No sooner had the last spoonful gone from bowl to prince than a lackey whisked away the former and old Rupert supplied his sovereign with a napkin the size of a beach towel. Sebastian made vigorous use of this linen sheet, but in point of fact I saw not the least besmirchment of his mouth after the furious bout with the elaborately garnished ice cream.

For a few moments after the withdrawal of the empty bowl Sebastian sat with closed eyes, his expression one of momentarily weary sweet sadness, suggesting the well-known postcoital effect, but then his eyes sprang open and he looked at me for the first time since I had sat down.

"It is probably not easy to accept the display you've just seen as not gluttony but a heroic effort to allay it."

"Indeed."

"By eating a sweet course as opener, one kills a good deal of the appetite for the rest of the meal," said the prince, earnestly compressing his several chins against his upper chest. "It's an American technique."

"Sounds like it," I could not forbear saying: I really had lost some of my awe of him after witnessing the foregoing scene.

"And the infantilism serves an emotional purpose," he went on. "Being royal is to be deprived of the warmer human feelings. You may not be aware of it, Mr. Wren. It was not my mother the queen who gave me suck, but rather a peasant wet-nurse whom I never knew, and I was reared by nannies and servants. In a word, that mound of ice cream topped with the preserved cherry might well represent the royal dug I was denied."

In America a grasp of basic Freudianism was now enjoyed by millhand and shopgirl: it was instructive for me to hear such platitudes from an absolute monarch.

I offered, "Or perhaps that of the wetnurse?"

Sebastian stared above my head. "No, the whipped cream and other embellishments would suggest a higher class." He fluttered his long lashes: he really had very nice eyes. "In any event it's a theory that derives from the studies of a certain professor who was not appreciated at the University of Vienna, but my great-grandfather saw the fellow's possibilities and brought him here. Froelich?"

"Or perhaps Freud, Your Royal Highness?"

Sebastian shrugged. "Perhaps."

"He became quite well known."

"For this theory of the substitute tit?" The prince smiled. "Is it not extraordinary what frivolous enterprises will succeed in the world beyond Saint Sebastian? My great-grandfather's interest in the professor was due to their common keenness for collecting classical antiquities and Jewish jokes."

At that moment Rupert rolled the trolley to the tableside, and I was pleasantly surprised to become aware that a footman was discreetly laying a place for me, with a plate bearing a gold relief of the crown, heavy gold cutlery, and a napkin of linen a good deal finer than any stuff I had worn against my skin: the serviette was embroidered with the crown, and the cutlery showed it in cameo.

On Rupert's trolley were several footed vessels the bowls of which were spanned by golden-brown domes of pastry. With a spoon from his dependent gear the old retainer broke through one of these and tasted whatever lay beneath, then put the bowl before Sebastian.

The prince scowled at it. "You old sod, you have spoiled the looks of this dish, as well as the surprise."

"A pity," said the imperturbable Rupert. "But I could hardly taste it without breaking the crust."

The prince seized a spoon and smashed the remainder of the pastry, churning the fragments into the contents of the bowl, which seemed to be a clear soup. He then dug into this mix with much the same urgency with which he had ingested the ice cream. He had emptied the first bowl by the time the lackey had placed mine before me, and before I penetrated the crust, Sebastian's empty vessel had been removed and Rupert had served a second order.

When I broke through the gossamer puff-pastry dome, I inhaled a celestial aroma which I could not have begun to identify until I saw, in the first spoonful of amber broth, black morsels of what could only be the priceless truffle, of which there were approximately as many pieces as there are noodles in a packet of my usual soup, Lipton Cup-a: I trust it is not bad taste to wonder what each of these bowls would have cost in New York.

Sebastian drained four or five of them into his gullet, and we did not converse during this performance, which had no sooner ended than Rupert returned with a trolley load of the largest poached salmon I had ever seen and a sauce in which at least a pound of beluga caviar figured.

It was during the fish course that I remembered that McCoy was not there. But it seemed impolitic to ask the prince about him, or indeed anything else, for with his last bite of the salmon, he turned eagerly to the new dish brought by Rupert, an enormous salver on which reposed dozens of tiny ortolans, which is to say birds the size of, uh, wrens: morally no different from cooked chickens, perhaps, or, speaking pantheistically, no more pitiable than a stringbean that has been boiled to death. Yet, this spectacle for me was fraught with pathos, and in fact I lost such little hunger as I had had.

Sebastian however seemed only just to be hitting his gustatorial stride with the small birds, seizing each by its hairpin legs and plunging it beakfirst into his mouth, biting it off at, so to speak, the little knees and discarding the legs of one en route to the next: quite a pile of these limbs began to accumulate alongside his plate. Apparently he could deal internally with the bones and beaks.

When a footman offered me a similar dish, I waved him off, but I did begin to sip the champagne I had been served by another.

Perhaps it was the diminutive size of what he was eating that reminded Sebastian of his own childhood. In any event, after the second dozen of the ortolans, he suddenly stared at me with misted eyes and said, "Like the old heirs apparent to the French throne, I was most savagely treated as a child. I was whipped bloody by my tutors, viciously slapped and pinched by my nurses, and the detestable old jackal who stands behind me at this moment was cruelest of the lot. My boyhood, Wren, was a living hell. It was intended to be, of course. That's the only sort of thing that develops the ruthless, vengeful qualities of character so necessary to a ruler."

"But now, Your Royal Highness, you need answer to nobody," said I.

"How wrong you are! Commoners never understand these matters," said the prince with a profound sigh. "I am in reality a helpless prisoner of tradition!" In a lugubrious manner he sucked two more little avian delicacies off their dead legs, but then quickly cheered up when more dishes arrived.

No doubt it would be as exhausting to read more of this meal as it was to sit there throughout it sans appetite. I couldn't have kept up with Sebastian at the most esurient moment of my hollow-bellied adolescence. I had no taste for the succession of dishes that arrived on the trolley, which never stayed long at rest: the game course (hare); the roast; the vegetables, which came in separate servings and included things like cardoons, salsify, baby artichokes no larger than plums; a profusion of salads; savories of cheese, mushrooms, bacon; and puddings and pastries and fresh fruits, each second or third course divided from the next by a palate-refreshing sherbet; and finally a great platterful of so-called *friandises:* bonbons, petit fours, candied chestnuts, and the like.

The prince said no more, seeming indeed to forget me as well as all else, in the transports of what could only be called his orgy, though again, as with the initial ice cream, he dropped or dripped nothing from his implements and, so far as I could discern, had not even a sheen of grease on his lips, which were thin for such a plump face. He did, when in the so to speak thick of things, breathe rapidly and stertorously, and his eyes when not rolling were closed.

How long this spectacle went on I cannot say, for though eating no more I continued to swallow champagne, my supply of which was ever replenished by my personal footman, but with little consequent peace of mind or, inexplicably, any reaction to the alcohol.

But I was taken by surprise when Sebastian ate a final chocolate cream, lowered his chin and produced a shattering belch, then, raising himself slightly, whitening knuckles on the ends of the chair-arms, flatulated even more loudly.

I tried to stick my nose into the champagne glass, but unfortunately it was of the narrow gauge called a flute. However, it might be of some interest here to note that the prince's farts were, in my limited experience of them, not noisome: explain that if you can without embracing the assumption that his bowels were as regal as his blood.

As the echoes of this report were still reverberating amongst the high vaultings overhead, Sebastian looked at me and said, "For some time now I have been bored with the affairs of state, from which a monarch cannot relieve himself short of abdicating. But I have no one to whom to turn over the crown. I am myself an only child. I have not yet married. By modern tradition the sovereign weds only a Sebastiani commoner. Until the late Renaissance we took wives or husbands from the other ruling families of Europe, but usually this meant that the consort was from a much larger and more powerful country than our little state, and too often it happened that the wedding was but a prelude to an attempt by the larger country to annex our land. We repelled all such, but at an awful price in Sebastiani lives. Sebastian the Eleventh was our Henry the Eighth, beheading as he did four queens in succession and all for the same crime: conspiring to betray their adopted country to the advantage of whichever German or Bohemian or Rumanian kingdom they came from."

The prince signaled to Rupert, and the old retainer brought him another glass of mineral water. He drank it down in one prolonged swallow, and then changed his position in the chair and farted again, this time producing a peculiar vibration that made the crystal glassware tremble.

"I know I should marry some healthy peasant," he resumed, "and impregnate her several times in succession, for my parents were irresponsible in producing only me—which is why I must take such precautions to ensure my safety: I am the last of the line. If I make no heir, this splendid little land will fall to the rabble."

Now, I am democratic to the marrow, and if I rail against the vile herd, or in any event that version of it all too oppressively evident in New York City, my objections have nought to do with matters of social class, my own being none too exalted. Yet, I confess that sitting at the prince's table, and more important, drinking his champagne, I was inclined to take his problem as having much the same value as he himself put upon it.

"Good heavens. Then you must by all means and with all haste find a bride, sir, for I have had my own personal experience with your enemies." I began to tell him about the Liberation Front bombing, but royalty has (or anyway this example of it had) small patience with the narratives of commoners, and Sebastian spoke as if I had been sitting in silence.

"Luckily," I was saying, "I took seriously the voice on the phone, and ran from my building, for—"

"The difficulty," said Sebastian, "is that I cannot endure the prolonged company of women. Unfortunately, tradition demands that the prince go through an elaborate series of wedding ceremonies, and then make at least some pretense of sharing his life with the princess, insofar as official functions are concerned."

"Aha," said I, in lieu of a better response. Obviously the prince was immune to charges of so-called sexism, which in New York were so easily brought by the kind of viragoes I dated, when my crime was so minor as to express a preference for a plain bagel as opposed to one of which honey, dates & nuts were constituents.

"I'm afraid that artificial insemination is not possible, owing to the many restrictions precedent places on the royal semen," said the prince. "The sovereign's spunk is considered virtually sacred. The sheets are burned if I have a nocturnal emission in bed, for example."

I drank a half-fluteful of champagne.

Sebastian was frowning into the middle distance. "I expect there's nothing for it but to get cracking, repugnant as my life will be thereafter, until there are sufficient children to make extinction of the dynasty unlikely, and then the princess might be dispensed with."

I choked on a draught of champagne. "She will be put to death?"

After a jolly laugh, Sebastian said, "No, that sort of thing has not been done in ever so long a time. It would now even be out of date to send her to a convent. No, she'll have a pretty villa in the country and an adequate staff: perhaps not sumptuous accommodations, but neither will they be mean. My own mother enjoyed such lodgings for many years."

I was so relieved to hear that he would not, when done with her, execute the poor woman who married him that I could respond almost blithely to the plight of his maternal parent.

"How nice."

"Rare indeed," said the prince, "is the great man who has not found a boy's flesh much sweeter than that of any female. Socrates, Caesar, Frederick the Great: there are few exceptions, and those who pretended otherwise were surely hypocrites."

To make some expression of what in the Aesopian jargon of those groups who seek to promote the acceptance of their own special tastes was called "freedom of choice" would be truistic to the point of lèse majesté under the current conditions: the prince hardly required my permission to pollute the choirboys of the country he ruled absolutely, not to mention that he was not misguided in finding many celebrated sodomites on the rosters of prominent men. But it was ludicrous to suppose that the likes of Napoleon, Mark Twain, and General MacArthur, to take a disparate lot, had been fraudulently hetereosexual. But remember that my purpose was not an inquiry into eroticism.

I drew on my store of trivia: "And England's Edward the Second and Ludwig the Mad of Bavaria." The prince frowned quizzically. I explained, "Two more for your list: I was responding to your theory with respect to great men."

Sebastian shrugged. "I am *always* right. Perhaps it's a pity. Sometimes I walk upon the palace wall and look down and see my subjects in the town below. I think how happy they are to be wrong in most of their opinions and judgments. How comfortable a lot, whereas I must carry the burden of perfect wisdom to my deathbed." He rubbed his hands together: I had not previously noticed how chubby they were; so fat were his fingers as to look as though inflated. He wore no rings.

He smiled at me and said, "But you do not yourself have a taste for boys."

"Yes, that is true, Your Royal Highness. I cannot explain it, but I seem to prefer women. It takes all kinds, I expect." I made a happy-go-lucky flinch. "Would you mind telling me how you knew?"

"*You are not a great man,*" cried the prince, preparing to chuckle. "And while the pederast has a keen sense of humor—he must have, given the joke he is perpetrating on nature!—he is usually the entertained and not the entertainer." He gave vent to his risibilities, with the sound of boiling water.

"Aha." Until one has been put in his place by a royal personage, one has not experienced the ultimate in that exercise: the difference in rank is so commanding that to be reminded of it is not offensive. The bootblack envies his busier colleague at the next stand, not the captain of industry in whose lobby he works. But the analogy is inadequate, for it is not impossible that a shoeshine boy can become a chairman of the board, whereas blood can never become blue by gift or effort. Thus far I had seen in Prince Sebastian not the ghost of an admirable or even decent trait, yet he was the reigning prince: not so long ago in the history of humanity, such a figure was believed to have been the personal selection of God and to be able, with a touch of his hand, to cure scrofula.

On the other hand, I was getting lots of free champagne and I felt an obligation to be companionable. "Uh, given this unhappy chore—that of marrying a person of the opposite sex—what would be your criteria for a prospective wife?" I smiled politely. "Should I come across a suitable candidate somewhere, perhaps back home." I had several ex-girlfriends I would have liked to sic on him.

"Americans? Oh good heavens, no!" he cried. "I cannot endure them. They speak in conundrums when they're young; when they're old, in homilies."

In my unsuccessful effort to understand that statement I concluded that I probably did, after all, feel the champagne more than I had realized. "Yes, well, perhaps you might tell me what kind of woman you would find least repulsive: blond, brunette, tall or short, full-bodied or slender, and so on?"

He had widened his eyes early in my list. "Obviously you are not aware that blonds are held in contempt in my country." He leaned back and snapped his fingers. The signal brought Rupert to the table. It occurred to me that this meal had gone on for hours, a long time for an old man to be on his feet. Sebastian merely breathed heavily in his direction, and Rupert drew a silken handkerchief from his sleeve, held it to the prince's nose, and Sebastian blew a blast that would have been as shattering as his flatulations had it not been so muted. When this episode was brought to a close, the ancient retainer wadded the cloth carefully and carried it out of the dining room.

The prince leaned confidentially towards me. "I wanted to get rid of him for a moment. He must go to burn the handkerchief that carries the royal snot. . . . The fact is, Rupert is not as young as he once was. He really makes a cockup of the job. I need a younger and more vigorous man. I could never trust any of my contemporary subjects." He slapped the top of the table. "Wren, would you like to be my principal body-servant?"

I pretended to ponder gravely on the matter, while my pulse raced in horror.

"Naturally," Sebastian went on, "I wouldn't expect you to perform all the duties done these many years by Rupert. You would not be required to attend me at stool, wiping my bum and so on, except in emergencies, midnight alarms, that sort of thing."

"Sir, you are too good."

He shrugged genially. "I am aware that times have changed, and that these warm, personal attentions that so characterized one's association with underlings in the past are now considered too quaint for words! One thinks something precious has been lost, but perhaps I'm hopelessly romantic. In any event, a lackey can always be found for the tasks for which you feel yourself too good."

"Sir, I—"

"No need to make up your mind on the instant," said the prince. "I can imagine how staggered you must be at the magnificence of the proposal. Here you are, an obscure tourist, a historical nobody, and without warning you are offered the opportunity to be as near a royal personage as anyone could be, short of a sexual partner, a role you can never play, owing to your advanced age."

I endeavored to rise above my disappointment at the limitations of the offer. "Indeed, sir, sire, I am overwhelmed. But might I ask about your earlier reference to blonds? They are despised in Saint Sebastian?" Experience has taught me that the most effective way to distract an unwelcome importunity of any kind is to ask a question.

The device worked with Sebastian. "Indeed they are," said he. "They are the butt of the typical Sebastiani joke. They must stay in their own areas at places of public entertainment, and are barred altogether from cafes and restaurants except those exclusive to themselves. They may pursue any profession, but usually they voluntarily confine themselves to the callings considered inferior by others, for example, the practice of law."

"Attorneys are blonds?"

Sebastian nodded. "You must understand that litigation is discouraged here, and that criminals are not allowed to have counsel. Thus a Sebastiani lawyer has virtually no work. His principal function is to provide a figure to be derided by those who have useful occupations."

"The first Sebastiani national I met was a blond young woman, as it happened. She is an airline stewardess."

"There you are," said the prince, waving his fat hand. "Politics is against the law here, of course, as is its brother profession, journalism, else they might make excellent pursuits for the Blonds, who by the way some years ago successfully petitioned me to command that their designation be spelled with a capital *B.* This was during the time of their Blond Pride campaigns."

Rupert had returned by now. The prince sneered at him and said, "You vile old creature. I've just offered your job to Wren. Now, what do you think of that?"

The venerable retainer remained dispassionate. "I think it's time for your nap. Tell this person to leave."

Sebastian laughed wrily. "Well, there you are, Wren. I'm afraid that ritual makes slaves even of princes."

I was not eager to remain. I lowered my champagne glass and stood up. "Thank you, Your Royal Highness, for everything. You can be sure I shall treasure this memory." This time I remembered to bow. I also thought I remembered that one was never to turn one's back on a monarch, that he who was departing must keep his front towards the person of kingly rank, bowing while walking backwards, all the way to the exit. I had doubts as to my ability to do this successfully on a route as long as the one that lay between my place at the table and the distant door through which we had entered this vast dining room.

I finally, boldly, presented the problem to the prince.

He pondered on it for a moment. "Why don't you go back for ten or fifteen paces, until you leave our immediate vicinity, after which you may discreetly turn and proceed on your way without giving the appearance of rejecting the sovereign." He looked at Rupert. "Wouldn't you say that might suffice?"

"Certainly not!" snapped the ancient retainer, standing behind the prince's chair. He had yet to address me directly.

Sebastian chuckled. "I could have predicted his reaction. Those who serve adore ceremony, which gives them something to do, you see. And they are overjoyed when the person in power is himself obliged to obey the commands of custom and tradition. Since he's done nothing all his life but abase himself before royalty, Rupert must believe that rituals are of the utmost importance, else he has wasted his life. Is that not so, Rupert?"

The old man remained expressionless.

I compromised and backed almost half the long way to the

door, going slowly so that I would not trip. In the anteroom I encountered General Popescu, who had presumably been waiting all this while, sitting in an uncomfortable-looking straight-backed chair.

On our way out to the gate I asked him whether he knew what had become of McCoy.

"I'm sure he's done what he usually does when he comes here," said the little general. "He goes to the royal wine cellars, finds a bottle or two, and empties them."

"The prince tolerates such behavior?"

Popescu's mustache moved. "He must. Any guest is protected by the immutable laws of hospitality."

4

McCoy was at the changing rooms, looking in better shape than had been his on our arrival. We got back into our proper clothes, reclaimed the car, and roared down the hill to town. The engine was too noisy for conversation, and McCoy was the sort of driver who drives as fast as the wheels can turn without losing their adhesion to the road.

Not far from the hotel we went through a square in the middle of which stood a pillory. My quondam enemy the concierge was fixed to it by wrists and ankles. Around his neck hung a wooden sign into which was burned the following legend:

I WAS RUDE

Before him a group of urchins, the first children I had yet observed in this country, were making what I saw only in a dumb show but were undoubtedly jeers and catcalls.

McCoy paid no attention to this spectacle. Arriving at the hotel, he scraped to a stop in the usual manner and left the car. But instead of entering the building he staggered several doors down the street and entered a shop identified on its front windows as the office of a cable service. From an inside pocket of the ancient jacket he took a sheaf of papers and presented it to the clerk, a balding person who wore rimless eyeglasses.

This man's acceptance of the manuscript was given reluctantly, with an audible sigh. "Mr. McCoy," said he, "I'm afraid—"

"You really should bill New York," McCoy said hastily. "I'm a mere wage slave of the imperialists." He threw up his arms, displaying infamous sweat-stains, and left briskly in the peculiar stride that looked as though it were but prefatory to a tumble but apparently never was.

Before I could follow, the clerk leaned on the counter in an attitude that I think was intended as beseeching and said, "I appeal to you, sir, as a countryfellow of Mr. Clyde McCoy! I am sorry to say he owes me a good deal of money. Several times a month he files lengthy cables to America, yet never does he pay me for transmitting them. He insists that I should bill the publications in reference. But when I do, my bills are ignored."

I crawl with shame when Americans bilk foreigners (while, with my cultured principles, shrugging it off when the swindle goes the other way, as it does mostly). "I'm no authority on the subject," I told him, "but he might well be right. I should think the *Times* or Associated Press or whomever he works for are honorable firms and would pay their debts. Perhaps you don't know the proper form for billing them."

The clerk frowned. "Those names are unknown to me." He peered at McCoy's latest manuscript. "This goes to *Crotch: The International Sex Weekly.* Is that printed by an honorable company?"

"I can't say I'm familiar with it," I confessed. But added quickly, "Which by no means implies that it does not enjoy respect in its field." I was drifting towards the door: I didn't want to get enmired in McCoy's problems.

"Perhaps," said the clerk, "you would kindly use your own influence to aid me in this matter. Be assured that in gratitude I will see that your own cable traffic is never interrupted."

Had I been better situated I might have upbraided him as an insolent puppy, for making a threat, but I had not forgotten that Rasmussen had furnished me with no money whatever.

I therefore lifted my finger to my brow, as if in affirmation, and was about to step out the door when, behind me, he added, "I will also introduce you to some pretty boys."

I stopped and turned. "No thank you, but perhaps you could tell me why since I arrived in your country it has more than once been assumed I am of the pederast persuasion?"

The clerk nodded briskly. "You see, female Blonds are everywhere available in Saint Sebastian. They are expected to give you their bodies. There's no romance in that state of affairs! But to have a boy is to violate nature, to partake of the forbidden. Now, that's exciting!"

"It's against the law?"

"Of course," said he indignantly. "What country would be so degraded as not to condemn the vile crime of sodomy?"

"What of the brunette women?"

"They're usually married."

"And no doubt adultery is considered a heinous crime—?"

"Except with Blonds, of course."

I went to the hotel, where a new concierge was behind the desk. In every way he seemed a twin to his predecessor, whom I had only just seen in the pillory, his gray-spatted shoes protruding through the lower apertures.

When I reached my room I found McCoy sitting on the edge of the bed. I soon learned, by asking him to leave, that it was his own room as well.

I asked incredulously, "You mean we're supposed to share it?"

His response was bitter. "*You're* complaining? It's my *home.*"

I looked around the walls and saw the wardrobe, the screen hiding the bidet and washstand, but nothing that could be considered personal possessions of his. The suitcase assigned to me had been placed on the floor.

"That's not even a double bed."

McCoy proved more thin-skinned than I expected. "You're none too fragrant yourself," said he. "May I suggest you take a long bath?"

"I'd like nothing better," I spat. "But where *is* the bathroom?"

"End of the hall, far right end. The WC's the other way."

"You don't have a private bath?"

"For God's sake, Wren, you think you're working for a profitable industry? Economy's the watchword these days. I can hardly keep body and soul together on what I'm paid—*when* I'm paid, that is, which at the moment hasn't been for months."

"And," said I, "they're always trying to cut appropriations further."

"They're not making much right now. At least that's their excuse."

"What does that mean? Graft or extortion money?"

McCoy frowned. "It means circulation is down and therefore

so is the income from ads. That's what they say, anyhow. I wouldn't know, being over here."

It occurred to me that we were speaking at cross purposes. "Aha," I murmured. "You mean that smut paper which provides your cover. I'm speaking of the Firm."

McCoy jerked his head indignantly. "OK, so they're easing me out in favor of a Johnny-come-lately like yourself, but do you have to be so damn superior? I was in Paris before you were born, junior. There was a time when I knew 'em all: Ole Ez, Gertie, Hem. I shared many a bottle of Jimmie Joyce's favorite *urine d'archiduchesse* with him: 'swhat he called a certain Swiss white."

I raised an eyebrow. "I thought you were World War Two. You're naming the Paris gang of the Twenties." His eyes rolled, but not in embarrassment. "I'm not displacing you in any sense," I went on. "I'm regularly a private investigator in New York. I'm just on temporary assignment here—without my consent, I might add. Rasmussen really shanghaied me."

"Don't know him," said McCoy. "Is he the new publisher?"

We were getting nowhere. "Forget about the porn!" I pleaded. "I'm one of you. I'm a fellow agent."

"I don't have the slightest idea of what you mean. I got a cable this morning from Mortie Rivers, managing ed. of *Crotch*, asking me to meet you at the airport and put you up for a few days. He didn't send any funds, needless to say, not even what they owe me, so this is the best I can do. I don't think it's nice of you to sneer."

I was touched by his appeal. "Forgive me," I begged. "I didn't mean to belittle your hospitality, which in fact has been more than generous. I wonder whether this 'Rivers' could be one of Rasmussen's masks?" McCoy continued to show puzzlement, so I finally had to say, "I know this is in execrable taste and as unprofessional as if a mobster were, with reference to his own associations, to use some term invented by the hacks of the communications media, 'Mafia,' or 'Cosa Nostra,' but I see no alternative to saying *CIA*."

"Who?"

"We work for it, don't we, you and I?"

"I didn't know there was such a thing in reality," said McCoy, whether disingenuously or not I couldn't say. "I always assumed the name was something invented by ex-Nazis when they transformed themselves into left-wingers. The genuine outfit was called the OSS. I never worked for it, but I understand they did a good job against the Krauts."

"That was during the Second World War," I said. I began to suspect that years of boozing had given him irreversible brain damage. But whether or not he would acknowledge it, he was my only local contact. "I thought I should compare notes with you on the prince."

"Why?" asked the veteran journalist.

"Well, for God's sake, he's the boss here, isn't he?"

McCoy shook his head. "Nobody pays any attention to him. He's stayed up there in the palace for years."

"He delegates his authority?"

"Naw. He doesn't have any real authority."

"Then who has?"

"Nobody," McCoy said. "Or maybe I should say, anybody who claims to have it—until of course it is challenged, as I did with the cops. Authority's usually just an idea, anywhere, except in those countries which maintain large standing armies for the purpose of policing their own citizens."

I was dubious. "Can't any individual then take the law into his own hands?"

"Maybe. But who would want to?"

I pondered on this for a moment. "Ambitious people."

"You won't find any of them here," said McCoy. "Money isn't used in Saint Sebastian. Everything's done on credit."

"Wait a moment. Just now the cable clerk complained to me about your overdue bill."

"That's because a cable goes out of the country, and foreigners want to be paid for their services." He thought for a moment, then said, "Hey, maybe that's why Mortie hasn't sent me any money for a long time. That little bastard ain't sending him my dispatches! Lend me a little something, willya, Wren?"

"Very funny," said I. "But tell me: are you serious? One doesn't pay for anything here but rather puts it on the tab?"

"That's why I came here during the war," McCoy said. "Went over the hill. That and the free cooze, of course, if you like blonds. Used to be a lot of ex-GIs here. The others all fucked themselves to death. Now you take me, I haven't got one up for several decades, and I consider myself the better for it." He stood up and uncertainly supported himself with a hand to the edge of the little table. "I just filed my month's work, Wren. I intend to relax for a while, wet my whistle somewhere in peace. I trust you'll take that bath before going to bed tonight. We'll be at awful close quarters."

I rose above the insult to ask a few more questions. Among them was why he wanted to be paid for his work for *Crotch* when he couldn't use the money except of course to pay for the cables?

"I import something decent to drink when I can afford it. The local schnapps is horsepiss."

"One more thing. Everybody here speaks English as a matter of course, but the self-characterized Liberation Front spokesman who phoned me a bomb warning in New York had a heavy accent that sounded Slavic. The stewardess on the plane this morning spoke English like a German. Is there a Sebastiani language?"

"How do I know?" McCoy growled impatiently.

"You've been here since World War Two and you can't answer that question?"

"I'd only *ask* it if I didn't know what they were saying," he told me, and staggered out the door.

What an intellectual loss he was. Unless of course that was part of his cover, which he maintained even when closeted with me. I decided to go out in search of more information about the country, but first I must spruce up my person.

In the valise that had been provided for me I searched without success for a bathrobe, then looked in the tall, dark armoire against the wall opposite the bed, which held what was presumably McCoy's wardrobe but could easily have been mistaken for a week's collection made by Goodwill Industries. I could find no robe here, either, but my colleague did possess (no doubt a souvenir of earlier, more ambitious days as a journalist) an ancient, stained trench coat. I stripped to the buff and donned this garment. My next search was for slippers or clogs or scuffs, something with which to protect my feet on the hike to the bathroom, but could find nothing suitable. McCoy owned several pairs of runover shoes, all wing-tipped and in a color that might be called pus-yellow, but they were too small for me. Finally I put on a pair of galoshes, which, large enough to go over shoes, could more than accommodate my feet.

Behind the catercornered screen that concealed the bidet and washstand I came upon the only towel on hand and a sliver of hard gray soap. So attired and accoutered, I went along the hall in the other direction from that which would take me to the elevator. My galoshes were buckled, and taking a leaf from the book of the old movie heroes, I had tied together the ends of the trench-coat belt.

The bathroom was at the farthest termination of the corridor, and so to speak camouflaged behind a closet full of mops and pails. From behind its locked door issued an extraordinary voice lifted in song. My initial annoyance at having to wait, in dirty trench coat and loose galoshes, while someone else soaked his hide for God knows how long, was soon assuaged by successive renditions of every familiar aria in the literature of the Italian grand-opera tenor: "Celeste Aïda," "La donna è mobile," "Vesti la giubba," and so on, in a Mediterranean extravaganza that went on, I should say, for the better part of an hour as I leaned against the slanted mops and brooms and listened to the golden sound. But at such times one does not tick off the minutes.

The bathroom door at last opened and, swathed in a crimson dressing gown made from sufficient cloth for Ringling's big top, an enormous man emerged. There was not enough room for the both of us in the mop-thronged anteroom, and I was forced to step backwards into the corridor. But I had been so enchanted by his magnificent voice that I did not resent this enforced courtesy.

I bowed as I backstepped. "Sir," I said, "that was the most extraordinary sound these ears have heard. Surely you cannot be a mere bathtub performer."

He shrugged in the classic Italianate manner. A thick white towel was around his neck, and he carried a striped sponge bag. His hair was covered with a bathing cap of pink rubber. The lower half of his face was all black mustache and beard.

His silence suggested he had no English. I therefore found

employment for the most useful of terms in my limited Italian vocabulary (one can go far on just these two): "*Maestro, complimenti!*"

Now he smiled radiantly and tossed his fat hand at a jaunty angle. He swept out and rolled down the hallway as if on parade-float wheels.

I entered a bathroom redolent of the subtle aroma of steam and the bolder scents of soap and cologne. The tub, mounted on high, gilded legs, was of heroic proportions—as it had had to be to hold its most recent occupant. Having taken off the trench coat, I sought a hook on which to hang it, but rare indeed is the sanitary facility, in America or Europe, which meets every simple need: so saith Wren's Law. Eventually I folded the garment into a parcel and placed it on the marble-topped dressing table, and there noticed, as I had not previously, that the other object thereupon was a tape recorder. The cassette inside it was labeled: "All-Time Greatest Hits of Enrico Caruso."

When I got back to the room after my bath, I found a rusty razor, a mangy brush, and a mug containing a cake of brothel-scented shaving soap, and I brought this ancient equipment into play, with ice water, to clean away a day's whiskers at the washstand behind the screen. I combed my damp-blackened hair (normally it is light brown) and donned a keen combo of synthetics: lime-green shirt; lavender trousers supported by a white plastic belt joined by an outsized brass buckle bearing the logo of Coors beer; the madras jacket, the fabric of which had the texture of crepe paper; and loafers made of cordovan-colored imitation leather.

I went down the hall and rang for the elevator. When the car finally arrived, however, it was filled to capacity by the enormous man who listened to Caruso while bathing. We now exchanged helpless but amiable shrugs, and I used the stairway.

I didn't know which of the twin concierges was at the desk, and decided I didn't care.

But he told me. "Mr. Wren, sir! I am now rehabilitated."

"It wasn't my idea that you be put in the pillory."

"It did me a world of good," said he. "And the institution also serves to meet the needs of youngsters, who, without the occasional malefactor to taunt and deride as he sits helplessly restrained, might torture animals or mutilate one another. As it is, we have little juvenile delinquency in Saint Sebastian."

"Indeed yours is a remarkable country," said I. "I wanted to ask you where I might go to find out more about it, whom I might interview—?"

He closed the lid of one eye, leaned across the desk, and spoke in a hoarse whisper. "The public library."

At this point the elevator finally reached the ground floor: unreasonably, it traveled more slowly with a heavier load than with a light one. The large man deboarded. I failed to mention earlier that he wore tennis clothes: V-necked white sweater, white linen shorts, white knee socks, and sparkling white sneakers. Again we exchanged gestures: this time a slight bow on my part and an inclination of the head, with a horizontaled forearm, on his.

I turned back to the concierge. "The public library?"

He put a fat finger to his lips, and virtually shouted in the direction of the large man, who was moving out the street door, a can of tennis balls in a rear pocket and dwarfed by the massive ham underneath, "A male brothel? But of course, my dear sir!"

"What are you doing?" I cried.

The door closed behind the vast figure of Caruso's fan. The concierge returned to his stertorous whisper. "We must be discreet."

"About the public *library?*"

He gave me a long stare, then threw up his fat hands. "Well, sir, if you are not concerned for your own reputation, then who I am to be worried?"

"Let me get this straight: there is something wrong with going to the library?"

He rolled the vein-webbed whites of his eyes. "Far be it from me to reflect on your tastes, sir, but you are an unrepresentative tourist. You have no apparent interest in sex, you are never drunk, loud, or abusive, and you've had only that one slight brush with the law, which I hasten to say was entirely the result of a misapprehension of mine."

"You mean that most visitors to your country act badly?"

He made his oiliest smile. "And why not? It's what we're here for."

I frowned. "Be that as it may, tell me how to get to the public library."

"Number Four, the Street of Words. The boy outside knows the way."

Though I didn't understand whom he meant, I went to the street. At the curb was a kind of rickshaw with a husky fair-haired young chap between the traces. He wore running shorts and a singlet in gold-trimmed blue.

"Please to tal me how to go, sair," said he.

I gave him the address and asked whether he had a sister.

"Many and brothers as well." His ingenuous broad face shone with good feeling. "You require dem for sex?"

"No thank you. Is one of the sisters named Olga?"

"Sure."

"Would she work for the Sebastiani airline?"

"Sure."

Wondering whether he might simply agree with anything asked of him, I climbed into the rickshaw's seat. He picked up the twin shafts and, swinging the vehicle around, headed uphill at a smart pace. Soon this became a trot: he was stronger than the engine of the ancient Minx I had driven when I was an impoverished young English instructor at State. Having reached the summit, we began to roll downhill at a greater rate of speed than the superannuated Beetle, for which I traded the Minx, could have attained under similar conditions. Such was our progress up and down several steep elevations.

Finally the young man, who was not even breathing heavily from his labor, turned into a little street narrow as an alley, lined with quaint little houses, some leaning at an angle, all decorated in Central European gingerbread, with miniature, one-man balconies attached here and there to the upper stories, and tiny shuttered windows like those in cuckoo clocks. He pulled me in front of the fourth house and lowered the traces, putting my seat at a downward angle from which it was simple to slide out. Despite the downhill speeds, I had felt secure in his hands, and the vehicle did offer a comfortable ride. At such a moment Saint Sebastian had much to recommend to a veteran of the choice of transportation evils available in New York City.

I walked to the somewhat undersized front door of the house

and knocked thereupon. In a moment it was opened by a slight, short man with very dark, intense, yet benign eyes.

"I'm sorry to trouble you," I said, "but can this possibly be the public library?"

"Indeed." He bowed and beckoned me to come in.

It was a strange library, however, judging from the entrance hall and then the front parlor of the house, which was furnished in a slightly shabby, old-fashioned bourgeois style, fringes on the lamps, tables with curved legs, and antimacassars on the ponderous overstuffed chairs. The only books in view occupied the four shelves of a relatively narrow cabinet with glass doors.

The volumes in this cabinet were of a uniform binding in dark green. I bent and read the dim gold lettering on the spine of the first: "*Encyclopaedia Sebastiana,* Volume I, A—Austria."

I asked the librarian, "May I?"

"Certainly."

I opened the uppermost of the glass doors and removed Volume I, opened it at random, saw the heading "Airplane," and began to read.

> AIRPLANE. The swiftest means of covering great distances in the shortest time. Its advantages over the bus, the train, and the various private vehicles are, in addition to speed, cleanliness, availability of toilets, and, strange as it might seem, according to statistics, safety; but it should be remembered that the normal passenger on an airplane never feels really secure. Most of us have our hearts in our mouths from the moment we take off until the landing is made, for though accidents might be rare statistically speaking, when one does happen, it's terrible, often resulting in hundreds of deaths . . .

I turned to the librarian. "Would you know who wrote the entries in this work?"

"Yes indeed. The original edition was a product of a committee of Sebastiani scholars at the turn of the century, but the *Encyclopaedia* is ever in the process of being revised."

"By contemporary scholars?"

The man's smile became smug. "The finest. Perhaps you would like to observe them at work? They are just upstairs."

With a certain eagerness I said I would, and he led me up a

narrow staircase to the next floor. I had expected here at least to see a collection of shelved volumes that might reasonably be called a library, but I encountered none in the room to which my guide conducted me.

This chamber, which fronted on the street, was furnished with a large table around which sat a dozen or so men, each of whom was reading in a green-bound volume of the sort that was in the bookcase downstairs. "Our visitor would like to learn how the *Encyclopaedia* is edited."

The nearest scholar smiled at me. "Quite simply, really. Every morning each of us picks out one of the books and reads in it until he comes to a passage with which he does not agree, and then, using a red pen, he rewrites that portion between the lines or in the margins, then tears the pages out and sends them upstairs to the typists, who prepare clean manuscripts for the printer."

"May I assume," I asked, "that in such cases you have come upon some information that is outmoded? Which must happen all the time with scientific subjects. For example, the entries on the exploration of space."

Another of the scholars chuckled. His fringe of hair was sandy in hue, and his spectacles were pince-nez from which dangled a grosgrain ribbon. "As it happens, we have no entry whatever on that subject, not having been able as yet to find anyone amongst us who knows anything about it."

A whitehaired man spoke up from farther along the table. "Perhaps *you* would like to do it."

"Me?"

"Or you might choose any other subject, if you don't want to do one from scratch, which can be quite taxing. I tried my hand at that as a young fellow, but soon gave it up. There was virtually nothing that interested me sufficiently to warrant the effort of writing an original article upon it. But revising what's there can often be very entertaining."

"Yes," I murmured. "You have interesting and, so far as I know, unique criteria for this enterprise. In the outside world, if I may use that term, scholarship is expected to be, anyway to have a go at being, objective. Yours would seem greatly conditioned by the personality, the character, of him who does it. Am I putting that fairly?"

"Yes, you are," said the whitehaired man. "But why are you concerned with being fair?"

I chuckled. "That's true. Why, indeed? I don't know any of you, and you all look utterly incapable of doing me either good or ill."

They all joined in good-natured laughter, and one of them said, "Be assured that we are absolutely inconsequential and that what we do has no value whatever. Only two copies of each volume are printed: one goes in the bookcase downstairs and the other is used up here. Furthermore, no one ever consults the downstairs set."

"No?"

"Well, if you think about it, why would they? The *Encyclopaedia* contains simply the arbitrary opinions of a number of individuals: anyone else's would be as good on any subject."

"Then of course," I said, "the question is obvious: why have such an encyclopedia?"

"The answer," the whitehaired man said genially, "is that we are the scholars of Saint Sebastian. What else could we do?"

I shook my head. "That's not as good an answer as you apparently believe it, sir. You might seriously pursue the facts, the truth, in the various areas of human enterprise, and record them, it, as carefully, as objectively, as possible."

"That sounds like more work than we have stomach for," said the sandy-haired man.

A watery-eyed scholar at the far end of the table cried, "It's great fun to be totally irresponsible, whereas being careful about truth is a dreary way to live." He bent over the book in front of him. "This is lively writing, much better than if lots of facts were given." He began to read aloud, " 'The tallest building in the world is a Woolworth five-and-ten in New York City. It's really tall, a whole lot bigger than any structure in Saint Sebastian. Big buildings are all right if you like to be way up high, but you might not care to live next door to one and have it block the sun from your roof all winter. But summer, now, that's another matter entirely. The shade provided by the skyscraper might be darned welcome.' "

I shook my head. "For at least half a century the Woolworth Building hasn't been the tallest, and it never was a five-and-dime. The person who wrote this entry apparently wasn't even aware of the Empire State Building, let alone the World Trade Center, not to mention a structure in Chicago that is taller yet. The other remarks, while perhaps true enough, are pretty obvious and banal, are they not? Are they really worth giving space to in the national encyclopedia?"

The whitehaired man looked at me in gentle reproach. "You do have strong opinions, sir. And forgive me if I say that you yourself are not without bias, are you? if you cannot name the tallest building because it's in Chicago and not New York. But I take it that your point remains that our encyclopedia might be inadequate?"

"With all respect, sir."

"And do you have a suggestion as to how we might remove that inadequacy?"

I sighed. They would have a massive job. "You might take a look at the *Britannica* or the *Larousse*, the *Brockhaus*, and so on. I don't think the *Great Soviet Encyclopedia* would be, all in all, much of an improvement on your own, but most of the major cultures have pretty good ones."

"These are already in existence?"

"Of course."

"Then why should we seek to duplicate what's there?" he asked.

I thought about this for a moment and had to admit to myself that I could find no reason, after all. "I'm sorry," I said. "I suppose what you do does serve the only need you have—and anything that does that, anywhere in the universe, can be said to be successful. . . . In fact, if I might accept your flattering invitation to contribute to your invaluable work of reference . . ."

"By all means, sir!" said the older scholar, and the others cried, "Hear, hear!"

"What I'm thinking of doing is an original entry." There were more sounds of encouragement.

I was taken by the librarian into a smaller, adjoining room, seated at a desk, and given a sheaf of quality foolscap and an old-fashioned fountain pen of the kind I had not seen since childhood. Its point glided across the heavy, creamy-textured paper as a keen blade skims over black ice. What I wrote was as follows.

> WREN, RUSSEL, born not so many years ago that he cannot still be called young, should be universally acknowledged as America's foremost playwright in the last quarter of the twentieth century, but in reality he has been infamously neglected by the *soi-disant* major critics, who however have some slight justification in that as yet his work has never been produced.

When I returned to the roomful of scholars and presented the little paragraph to the man with white hair, he read it eagerly and then, with every sign of approval, gave it to the man next to him. When this second reading had been completed, the two nodded at each other.

"Superb!" said the older man. "We are delighted. But I must point out that it is, after all, a revision of an existing entry."

"How can that be?"

He bent over the volume before him, flipped through the pages until he had arrived at the one he could use as evidence, and handed the book to me. "See for yourself."

It was midway along the right-hand page, in the *W*'s, between Sir Christopher and a bird called the Wren-Tit:

> WREN, RUSSEL, a shabby private detective in New York City who poses as a playwright to gain sexual favors from women and bluff his fellow man.

"So you see," said the elderly scholar, "you have provided an obviously much needed revision."

"I don't suppose you could tell me who composed this entry," I asked, tapping the book with an offended forefinger.

He looked around the table. "Anyone here?" But they all of them shook their heads in negation.

At length a skinny man with a prominent wen on his nose pursed his lips speculatively and said, "That wouldn't have been Mr. McCoy?"

"Perhaps," said the whitehaired man. "He's done most of the American entries, for obvious reasons."

"Good heavens," I cried. "You people unwittingly took quite a chance. I assume you didn't know that McCoy had AIDS."

But my spite went for naught. They had never heard of the ailment despite the local prevalence of buggery.

The slight, dark librarian then conducted me to the third floor, where a battery of male typists made manuscripts of the revised entries for the encyclopedia.

My guide told me that these were regularly taken by himself to the royal printing house. He went now to a metal strongbox, painted bright red, on a table near the door, opened its hasp, and peered within.

"Filled. We might go there now, if you'd care to come along."

Outside, I suggested we take the rickshaw, which was waiting at the curb, for the seat was wide enough to accept the slender man along with me, and the blond in the traces was certainly strong enough to pull the two of us. But my guide told me the printer was just along the street a few steps away.

The printer's shop proved to be in an outbuilding, originally no doubt a stable, behind the house at the end of the street. A large hand-operated press, glistening disc cocked at the traditional angle, dominated the room, and sawdust covered the floor. A stocky man in an inky apron and a handmade paper hat was setting individual pieces of type in a composing stick: he did this with remarkable speed, plucking what he needed from a shallow horizontal box of pigeonholes.

"That's nice to see," I told my guide. "When I was a boy there was still a fellow in my town who did job printing on a hand-powered press when he was not occupied with Linotyping the weekly paper. By the way, do you have a newspaper in Saint Sebastian?"

"Broadsides," said he, "when the occasions present themselves, but not on a regular schedule of any sort. Is it true that elsewhere in the world, newspapers are published every day and at the exact same time of day, whether or not there is anything of note to report?"

"And television and radio newscasts, as well," said I, "relentlessly. And weekly magazines and papers, in addition, though of course by the time a week has passed, it would be unusual were nothing to have happened."

He shrugged. "No doubt the problem is frequently addressed by invention."

"That does happen at times, but if they're caught at it there's hell to pay." I saw him frown, and added, "But perhaps the practice is routine in Saint Sebastian?"

"It surely would be, but we do not bother with news in the first place, you see."

His smugness irked me. "But you do bother with an encyclopedia."

"It cannot bother many if only one copy is available for reading, and of course we do what we can to keep quiet about the existence of a public library."

The printer was now locking up a chase in which many sticks of type had been brought together to constitute a page. After the fashion of craftworkers everywhere, he found it easy to ignore laymen.

"Yes," said I, "and I confess I cannot understand why, unless the idea is simply to keep the populace in a state of ignorance. In which case there would be no sense even to have something called a public library."

"The idea, I should say, is rather to make it necessary to expend some personal effort in relieving one's ignorance," he told me. "Not to force-feed information to the reluctant."

There might have been some sense in this had a genuine library been at the end of the obstacle hunt, or even one encyclopedia of substance and not such a farcical product as was being fabricated by the scholars of Saint Sebastian, but as a guest in the country I did not make these points aloud.

The printer finally turned. He winced at the sight of the red box. "That's not filled *again?*"

The librarian cringed and said apologetically, "Well, that's our job, isn't it?"

"Speak for yourself," the printer growled. Then he stared at me and asked rudely, "Who's this one?"

"I'm from New York," I said, choosing from amongst my various identifications (nationality, profession, religious preference, etc.) the one I supposed would make the quickest impression on a national of a tiny foreign country.

But I immediately lost the advantage.

He demanded, "Where's that?"

"*New York?* Why, in America. You've heard of America."

"Don't be insolent," said the printer. "What's new about it? Where's Old York?"

"England. But the Old isn't nearly as well known as the New."

"I don't like new things of any kind," said he. "They're never really reliable, no matter what you say. Would you consider this new place as more reliable than the old one?"

"Certainly not. But is that a reasonable criterion?"

The printer cleared his throat angrily. "Name a better one! If you go about irresponsibly naming things 'New,' then you should expect to defend the practice sooner or later. You say New York is well known. For what?"

For no good reason I was altogether on the defensive, and when my back is to the wall, like most people I resort to dollars and cents. "Money! I understand you don't use any in Saint Sebastian, but please believe me when I say that elsewhere it makes the world go round, with the exception of totalitarian-collectivist lands, where brute force, realized or implied, would seem to be the catalyst."

The printer resituated the paper hat on his head. "Do you have a lot of money?"

"As it happens I have very little."

"Why, when you live in its capital?"

"Aha," said I. "That is a somewhat rude but not irrelevant question. I always expect to be given some in the future. A play written by me might have a great success, making me a rich man overnight."

He thought about this for a moment. "And life as a rich man would be to your liking?"

"I assure you it would, not because I yearn for possessions. Indeed, I might even own fewer things than I do now—or did before my home was destroyed. Incidentally, that was done by extremists from Saint Sebastian, so not everyone here thinks this country is a paradise." Going on the offensive made me feel better.

He simply ignored my later point and focused on the earlier. "What would being rich do for you?"

I welcomed the opportunity to sort out my feelings on that subject. "Services! One could hire people to take clothes to the cleaner's and to wait until the machines were free at the Laundromat. . . . Just a moment: if you were rich enough, you could wear clothes until they were soiled and then simply throw them away and send your flunky to the shops for more. Having one's own chauffeur-driven limousine would be basic, but what of getting from your apartment to the car? Such a routine journey can be fraught with discomfort and even danger in New York. With money one could hire a team of bravos to carry one to the curb! These same men, preferably conspicuously fearsome-looking plug-uglies, would accompany one everywhere and forestall, by their appearance alone, most of the abuse which is a quotidian feature of life in the city: the vicious responses of cabdrivers to imaginary encroachments; the thrusting shoulders of sidewalk thugs; the threats of those who find you, if unarmed and harmless, the principal author of their social disenfranchisement; and even the fishwifery of well-upholstered matrons who cannot forgive you for falling victim to their umbrella-tips. In restaurants such bullyboys could command the attention of the same blind-and-deaf waiter who is hired specially by one eatery after another, whichever you choose to dine at that day, to serve cool steak and warm ice cream, to bring Bulgarian claret and charge you for Mouton, and to replace a greasy fork with one which displays dried marinara sauce."

The printer was staring at me with a raised eyebrow.

"Mind you," I went on, "there are free radio psychiatrists, and museum food has got more elaborate in recent years, and at certain gathering places notables are sometimes to be glimpsed, trading gossip and/or punches, and one who's fascinated by fresh-made pasta and picketing against gentrification need never be lonely."

The printer shook his head. "It's obvious you suffer from an exaggerated case of envy. You lust for what you cannot have, and envy has vitiated such force as you might originally have had. My advice to you is to settle in Saint Sebastian and learn and practice a craft: printing, if you like. I can always use an extra apprentice. Or carpentry, shoemaking, masonry, cooking or baking, distilling schnapps, brewing beer. There's plenty to do, none of it characterized by the hateful competitive strife typical of, by your account, your home principality."

I passed up the opportunity to quote the legendary bon mot of the circus employee who gave elephant-enemas, "And leave show business?" I simply told him I'd think about it, thanked him, and left.

On his own exit the librarian, who I now decided greatly resembled the author of *In der Strafkolonie*, had plucked, from a pile near the door, a copy of a one-sheet newspaper.

I asked him, "Is that a broadside?"

"Yes, indeed," said he, presenting it to me.

It bore a headline of modest size: "The Case Against Training Birds to Speak." I read it aloud, and asked, "Is that a current problem here?"

"At least one person thinks so," said my companion, "else he would not have written this."

"The subject is characteristic of the broadsides?"

"I'd say so. Natural history is a favorite topic. There was one last week that considered what might happen if mice were as large as pigs."

I lowered the paper. "Have you ever heard of a long story entitled *Die Verwandlung?*"

"No."

"Have you ever read *I Promessi Sposi*, the *Thesmophoriazusae*, *Gammer Gurton's Needle*, *Wilhelm Meisters Wanderjahre*, Ghalib's ghazals, or, for a change of pace, the frothy entertainments of the late Thorne Smith: *The Night Life of the Gods*, perhaps, or *Topper Takes a Trip?*"

"Never."

"I suspected as much. It is no doubt desirable in Saint Sebastian for a librarian to be—forgive my candor, which is intended to be scientific, not abusive—to be, in a word, ill read."

"I'm quite illiterate," said he, with a smile I should have called proud. He nodded at the paper in my hand. "I can't read a word of that."

"Uh-huh. And it doesn't strike you as strange to have such employment as you do?"

"Not at all. You see, I am therefore utterly unbiased. One book is as good as another to me."

"You don't really have many books at the library, do you?"

"Not now."

"At one time there were more than the *Encyclopaedia Sebastiana?*"

"A good many," said the librarian. "I gave them all away."

The rickshaw man was waiting at the curb. His head was down and he seemed to be dozing as a horse might in the same situation.

"To whom did you present them?"

"I gave one to each person, but sometimes, when I was told that several constituted a set, I gave those that belonged together to the same person, relying on his honesty, for of course I was unable to identify the titles except by ear."

"Extraordinary," I said. "And may I ask why you disposed of the collection of the public library of Saint Sebastian?"

"It seemed to make little sense to keep all the books with me, who could not read, when they might each find a good home with someone who would make use of them."

"Yes, but people generally do not reread the same volume constantly unless it's a religious scripture and they are fanatically devout," I told him. "Most readers go from one book to the next."

He was shaking his head. "Not in this country."

"Come now, you don't mean to say a Sebastiani reader remains with the *same* book?"

"With all respect," said the librarian, "if your practice is otherwise. But my literate countrymen believe that, going from one book to another, the reader can never get more than the most superficial sense of what the author has taken the pains to write."

I was not insensitive to the point being made, having myself in my pedagogical days taught a survey-of-world-lit. course at State, in which in the space of barely eight months the students were obliged to pretend they had read the major works of some twenty centuries (I confess their instructor had to fake a few himself). "There is much to be said for that argument if the books concerned are masterpieces," I noted. "But *every* volume in the library? Would you not have had some titles of negligible value: the mendacious memoirs of film stars, the apologias of ex-statesmen, once famous muckrakings made pointless by time, first-aid manuals for personality disorders now out of fashion, and the kind of narratives our forebears found risqué but which nowadays would anesthetize with ennui a novice nun?"

"Sebastiani readers do not make such distinctions," said the librarian. "If a book is printed and bound, it's good enough for them."

It occurred to me to ask, "Would the books concerned have been the work of Sebastiani authors?"

"Indeed they would," said he.

"Might it be possible for me to meet one or more of your writers? There are some extant?"

"Certainly. The pink house just there is their quarters." He indicated the building next to the library.

"When you say 'quarters,' do you mean they live there in a kind of colony?"

"Of course. That is the law."

"When you say 'law,' do you mean that they are obliged to live there?"

"Not unless they want to practice that profession," said the librarian. "No man can be forced to become a writer, but if he does become one, he must live here and not amongst the populace."

"What is the purpose of that law? For whose benefit was it enacted? The public's or the writer's?"

"Both, I should think," the little librarian said. "Thus neither is polluted by the other."

"I'm not sure what that means. By 'polluted,' do you mean—"

"I'm sure it's a fancy way of saying 'bored,' don't you know," said he. "But here we are." We had reached the doorstep of the two-story building in pink stucco. "The authors will be having their . . . let me see, which meal will it be? Breakfast, Postbreakfast, Lunch, ah yes, this would be Postlunch without a doubt. I'm sure you will be most welcome in the dining room."

5

We entered the pink house and went upstairs to a dining room that occupied most of the second floor. Its central feature was a large round table, at which about dozen men, one or two young, one or two old, but most of them in middle age, sat silently drinking what would seem from its color, and the shape of the glasses, to be sherry.

"Gentlemen," said my sponsor, "you have a visitor from New York. I know you'll want to make him welcome."

One of the writers, a flabby-cheeked individual with the melancholy eyes of a hound, gestured with his forefinger. "There's a place there, next to Spang."

I assumed it was Spang, a sallow, longlipped man, who moved so that I might slide into the chair beside him. But when I said, "How do you do, Mr. Spang. I'm Russel Wren," he replied, in a high-tenor voice, "Oh, I'm not Spang. I'm Hinkle."

"Since when are you not Spang?" asked the sad-eyed man who had first spoken to me.

"I've never been Spang. He's deceased."

"If that's so, then why have you never mentioned it before?"

"There's never been an occasion to do so," said Hinkle. "You've never called me Spang before."

"But *I've always thought you were Spang.* Can't you get that through your thick head? Simply because I've never had to use your name before doesn't mean that I was not certain what it was."

"Well, what do you want me to do, for God's sake?" Hinkle asked. "Change it to Spang so that your usage is legitimized?"

The flabby-cheeked man smirked. "Well, aren't we getting toplofty?"

I looked towards my neighbor on the left, but he did not return the favor. He was a beetle-browed sort, with a hard-looking jaw. He stared malevolently into his sherry.

No one did anything about getting me a glass. The librarian had taken a silent leave.

I began, "You see, my own work has been for the theat—" but was interrupted by a curly-headed author across the table, one of the younger men.

"Leave it to you assholes to make an issue of something so inane. Who cares who's Spang and who isn't?"

Hinkle said, "You wouldn't be happy if someone got your name wrong, Boggs."

"I couldn't care less!"

"All right, then, I'll call your bluff. From now on, I'll refer to you as Sprat."

The curly-haired man frowned. "Now, wait a minute. That's insulting. I don't have to take that sort of thing."

"You phony," Hinkle growled in disgust. "It's simply a name I made up out of the blue. What's insulting about it?"

"It's the name of a tinned fish, as you very well know!"

Some of the others were sniggering now. A well-constructed young Blond waitress appeared behind a serving cart full of soup bowls. She began to distribute the soup, starting with me, then moving on in a counterclockwise direction towards Hinkle.

"You're being oversensitive, Boggsy," said a man whose dark hair was plastered flat to his scalp and parted in the middle. "My name is Merkin, but I've never been embarrassed by it. It was good enough for my old dad and it's good enough for me."

"Of course that's an archaic word," said the only man yet to have addressed me, *viz.*, he who had directed me to a seat. "You'd feel different if you were called Cunthair. I think Boggs has a point."

"Well," said Merkin, " 'bog' meant 'shit' in the olden time, did it not?"

Someone else asked, "Verb or noun?"

I saw with astonishment that the large-nosed author next to

Hinkle had slipped his left hand up under the skirt of the waitress as she bent to place his soup before him, and was obviously massaging her buttock. No one but me, including the young woman, paid any attention to this.

When I looked again at Boggs, he was plucking up a roll. He proceeded to hurl it at Merkin. Merkin with amazing speed lifted a fending palm, and the roll bounced off it and soared to fall into the soup which the waitress had placed before the large-nosed man while he was fondling her behind.

The victim seized the nearest basket of rolls and began to hurl them one by one at Boggs, who ducked some but was hit by several. When the fusillade had ended, Boggs asked the man next to him to pass the boat-shaped glass dish that held olives, black and green, and sticks of celery.

The author with the flabby cheeks protested. "Now, hold on, Boggs. I'm fond of olives and don't want to eat them off the floor."

Boggs carried the dish to this man and emptied it on his head. "Eat your fill, then, Buzzle."

The waitress had now reached the man on my left, but the cart was empty. There had been just enough bowls for each of the regulars. My presence had thrown off the count. With an extended finger she enumerated the bowls she had served, shook her head, and burst into tears.

Buzzle had been furiously gathering up as many of the olives and celery sticks as he could, after they had rolled and bounced off his head, no doubt with an angry intent to launch them at Boggs, who had returned to his seat, but the weeping girl distracted everyone for the moment.

Hinkle was first to speak. "You idiot," he cried to her, and then he shook his head at various of his colleagues and even at me. "It's an outrage that almost every day our meal is marred by some stupidity on the part of that Blond." He addressed her again. "You fool!"

She sobbed into her hands and then peeped out with two blue eyes. "Is brinkink twelf as alvays."

Merkin shouted, "Count them, you silly bitch!"

When she did as instructed, most of the writers joined her in pointing at the bowls and announcing the numbers aloud, in chorus. They arrived at twelve.

"I don't understand it," said Hinkle. "There *are* enough bowls." They repeated the process, this time without being joined by the waitress, who stood silent and humble alongside her cart.

I finally said, "May I explain? You see, I am the ex—" At this point Buzzle hurled two handfuls of olives at me, and Merkin began to pelt me with rolls. I was also the target of odd names as terms of abuse: "Barber!" "Dentist!" "Accountant!" And so on.

For a moment I was taken aback to be so treated when I was supposed to be their guest, and I crossed my arms across my face and sank beneath the table, out of the line of fire. But then, since I hadn't really been hurt, indignation soon became my dominant emotion. I came up fighting. I lifted my bowl and hurled the soup across the table into Boggs's face. I picked up from the floor some of the rolls thrown at me and fired them at Hinkle, Merkin, and Buzzle. I snatched up olives and celery and dashed them into the face of the grumpy-looking man on my left, though in truth he had not been one of the aggressors against me.

"You shits!" I cried. "You call yourselves writers?" Perhaps this had nothing to do with the issue at hand, but surely one need not justify what one says when exercised.

Eventually it struck me that from the moment I went on the offensive, the authors became peaceable, and by the time I had committed several acts of violence against them they had begun to assume expressions I could not but identify as admiring, perhaps even downright obsequious. For example, the man on my left wiped his face with a napkin, rose, and came meekly to me.

"Sir," said he, "please accept my apology for having offended you as apparently, though without intention, without indeed having, to my memory, been aware of your presence until this moment—unless, to be sure, it was that very ignorance for which you gave me what was surely a merited punishment and if not was yet no doubt deserved according to that principle enunciated by the Bard, *videlicet,* which amongst us could escape the noose were justice to be honored more in the observance than the breach?" He offered his hand. "Your servant, sir. I am Barnswallow."

"Wren," said I. I transferred to my left hand the roll I had been holding and shook with him: he had a weightless but clinging sort of grip, which one half expected to have to scrape away.

"Welcome to our little convocation," he said. His paunch hung over his belt. It now occurred to me that all these authors wore matching navy-blue three-piece suits, most of which were rumpled, stained at the vest, and sprinkled with dandruff at the shoulders and even the lapels. Barnswallow was one of those whose vests were unbuttoned so as to offer a modicum of liberty to their extra flesh.

Hinkle was next to offer his welcome. The others around the table were beaming and intoning, "Hear, hear."

I finally lowered my roll to the tabletop. I was not yet prepared to be extravagantly genial, but I did say, grudgingly, "Well, all right, I suppose I can accept the apology. But I'll strike back if I am the recipient of any more aggression. I realize I am an uninvited guest, but you might simply have asked me to leave."

"Excuse me, Mr. Wren," said Hinkle. "It would have been rude by our lights to ask you to go, you see. As it was, we proved you were welcome by treating you as badly as we treat one another!"

Again the "Hear, hear"s were sounded around the table.

"All right," said I. "I'm willing to put the misunderstanding, if such it was, behind me. Now please resume your usual activities. I assume these lunches are normally the occasions for discussion of your works in progress?" I sat down now, as, following my lead, did those writers who had sprung up earlier.

"Actually," said Boggs, across the table, after the chair legs had stopped squeaking, "we talk almost exclusively about inconsequential matters, as it happens. Never do we mention to any of our colleagues what we're working on at the moment, lest he steal the idea and complete the work before the man can whose original idea it was."

"Then you don't trust one another?"

Buzzle snorted. "Certainly not! We writers are the most unscrupulous people in the country. We're well known for that.

Not only will we steal one another's ideas. We mingle with the crowds in the marketplace, shoplifting and picking pockets. If someone is still naïve enough to invite any of us to dinner, we'll swipe what we can: silverware, family heirlooms small enough to slip into a pocket, dirty underwear from the bathroom hamper—"

"Male or female underclothing?"

"Either," said Boggs. "As long as it's been worn recently."

Whether or not I was supposed to take him seriously, I decided that these were the most unattractive people I had met thus far in Saint Sebastian. Indeed, the Blonds, though cretins, were, all in all, the nicest. When I went on the attack, the waitress had slipped out of the room. Now I espied her peeping from the swinging door that obviously led to the kitchen. I had not previously seen her face straight on: it bore a notable resemblance to those of Olga and Helmut.

When she determined that the soup course was so to speak over, though most of it had been splattered across the table, she re-entered the dining room, transporting, with high-held wrists, a large trayful of loaded plates. So as to keep the peace—for despite their avowals of friendship I did not trust this lot—I waved off the dish she was about to place before me.

"You don't care for roast stoat?" asked Hinkle. "They can probably rustle you up something else, then: perhaps some of yesterday's badger."

"Actually, I've already eaten and within the hour," said I. "I shouldn't have taken the soup. But please go ahead, all of you. I'm here as an observer. Don't mind me."

I cannot justly complain, for I had told them to proceed, but I must say they fell to their plates with an ardor, even a ferocity, that astonished me. For a few moments the table was a mise-en-scène of flashing cutlery and gnawing teeth. Juice dripped from chins, fragments of food fell from flying forks. Boggs's knifework was so savage as to wound his index finger, and his blood dribbled to join the other fluids staining the tablecloth. With closed eyes one would have heard a troop of hyenas demolishing a carcass. Before I had completed an ocular circuit of the company, those first served were displaying empty plates.

I addressed Hinkle, who had long since devoured the last morsel of his own portion. "You fellows are quite the trenchermen. Do you work up such appetites at writing?"

He patted his protuberant belly. "I've never made up my mind about the chicken or the egg: maybe gluttons are naturally attracted to the profession, for some reason. If so, bless me if I can see the connection."

The waitress was now going around with red wine. After every four persons, she began a new bottle, for the glasses were large and she filled them to the rims.

I asked, "Do you people drink a lot?"

"Not during the week, except after eleven A.M." said Hinkle, lifting his goblet and emptying it in one long draught. When he lowered the glass he looked around for the waitress. She was detained. Barnswallow's hand was between her legs.

"And sex?"

"Yes," said he, "with anything." He gestured with his glass at the waitress.

"By the way, don't you have any female authors in Saint Sebastian?"

"If you can call them that. They write nothing but pornography."

"Are you serious?"

"Is that so surprising, given the filthy imagination of the typical woman?" Hinkle was now growing annoyed with the failure of the waitress to fill his glass, but Barnswallow was working ever more furiously under her skirt, to which activity she seemed indifferent, whereas he was gasping stertorously. It was an ugly spectacle to me, but his colleagues were seemingly oblivious to it.

I wasn't eager to start more trouble, so I made gentle application to Hinkle.

"It isn't her fault. Why don't you ask Barnswallow to unhand her?"

Hinkle shrugged. "We're never critical of one another in such a situation."

"You were only just throwing things and insulting each other!"

"That was only personal," said he. "This is principle. Can't you see that? A Blond's a Blond!"

I turned in my chair, so that I could not see Barnswallow from the corner of my eye. "I suppose it's none of my business. . . . Tell me, what do you write?"

"I do children's books. Each of us has his own specialty. Boggs for example does books and articles explaining how things happen in the natural sciences: how the porcupine throws its quills, how the basilisk paralyzes its intended prey with a fixed stare, and so on. Buzzle's latest work is a series of profiles of three great men who were afflicted with chronic diarrhea: Mohammed, Molière, Marx."

I frowned. "Just a moment. Can that be true? How does he—"

Hinkle made a superior smile. "Pure assumption. Else we *couldn't* say, according to Buzzy. Molière, for example, was awfully cunning at it, leaving not a shred of evidence."

"Neither, I should imagine, did the other two. Also, I happen to remember from my scouting days that a porcupine certainly does not throw its quills, and that a basilisk can paralyze with a glance is a quaint old delusion of the Middle Ages, if I recall the footnotes in my college edition of Shakespeare."

At this point Barnswallow finally released the waitress. She came to Hinkle with the wine bottle.

I asked her for her name.

"Inga."

"You're not by chance related to Olga and Helmut?"

Her answer did not take me by surprise. "Sure."

Hinkle was not offended by my negative comments. Still smiling proudly, he went on. "Hozenblatt, over there, is our modern historian. He is best known for his comprehensive study of the concentration camps in which the Jews exterminated the German and Austrian Gentiles, 1938 to '45. Currently he is at work on a book in the same vein, this one concerned with the Siberian forced-labor camps in which anti-Communist zealots confine benevolent secret policemen."

I retrieved one of the overturned sherry glasses and asked Inga to fill it with table wine. "Thank you," I told her, and added, sotto voce, "I'm your friend."

She made her blue eyes into veritable saucers and asked in a loud voice, "You vant to screw?"

But no one, including Hinkle at my other elbow, showed any

sign of having heard this. I still had not got used to the utter lack of sexual shame in Saint Sebastian.

"No, thank you," I told Inga, and turned back to the writer of children's books. "Tell me, Hinkle, what kind of thing do you write about for kids?"

He was pleased by the question. "All manner of informative subjects, actually, from economic theory to contraception. Then, on the entertainment side, surveys of nightlife around the world, the *caves* of Paris, the after-hours joints of New York, the transvestite bars of Istanbul, and so on."

"And do the children understand this material?"

"Well, of course, *nobody* understands economics," said Hinkle. "I expect they get some profit from the rest of it. But if they don't, what does it matter? They're just kids."

"Some of you have British-sounding names: Merkin, Boggs, *et al.*, and everybody in the country speaks fluent English, though so far as I know, you're a considerable distance from Great Britain."

Hinkle narrowed his eyes. "You're not speaking derisively, are you?"

"Certainly not!"

"Because an awful lot of people do, if they know you're an author. Which is why we all of course use pseudonyms, some of which are British. As to the use of the English language throughout the country, you'd have to look in the *Encyclopaedia Sebastiana* for the whys and wherefores. But my understanding is that at some time in the early nineteenth century the then reigning prince decided to simplify the matter of language, the choice of which in conversation had become trendily arbitrary. It was chic, especially among the better class of ladies, to address a person in an exotic tongue. The other would of course endeavor to one-up the first by replying in an even more obscure language. The universal use of English seemed the answer, for what is it but a compound of many other tongues, beginning as German, taking on Latin from the Romans, then French from the Normans, and so on, and eventually even collecting such exotica as *pajama* from Persian by way of Hindustani and *goober* from Bantu?"

During the course of the foregoing remarks I had emptied my

glass. I rose now and pursued Inga, who was at the turn of the table with her bottle. While she poured, I was addressed by the nearby Hozenblatt.

"I say, Wren, perhaps you could settle this argument I'm having with Smerd. I maintain that Montenegro is a peak near Kilimanjaro in Africa, whereas he insists it's a very dark wine of the Jura. What do you say?"

"Neither. He was a Latin American singer of the bossa-nova era, now almost forgotten."

Smerd was a husky, powerful-looking man, whose constant expression seemed to be a scowl. I asked Hinkle what sort of thing Smerd wrote.

"He's our muckraker. He exposes people, often literally, as when he's researching the prevalence of dirty feet. He's not above knocking you to the ground, tearing off your shoes and socks, and prying your toes apart, looking for toe jams."

I glanced again at the author in question, but my eyes were attracted to a man on his left, a big fat jolly writer with a high-colored face and watery eyes. He had taken the bottle away from Inga, a new bottle, and putting its mouth to his, lifted its base into the air.

I asked Hinkle who that was.

"Riesling," said he. "Our literary critic."

When I looked again at Riesling I saw him emptying the bottle unto the very last drops, to catch which, on his protruded red tongue, he held the neck perhaps a foot overhead. Then without warning he hurled the bottle at Merkin, who however caught it easily. Riesling roared-wept with laughter.

"No doubt, despite his jovial appearance, he wields a savage pen?"

"Not at all," said Hinkle. "He writes only praise."

"Surprises keep coming," I said. "What kind of thing does he write about?"

"Poetry is his great specialty."

"There are many Sebastiani poets?"

"Not one," Hinkle said.

"How's that?"

"Riesling writes essays, even long books, about great poetry that has never been written."

"Nobody ever tries to write poetry?"

"They'd keep it a secret if they did," Hinkle said with feeling. "Riesling had sworn to murder anyone who tries. Even Smerd, strong and brutal as he is, is scared of Riesling in that regard."

My second glassful was now gone. I twitched a finger at Inga, and when she came to me with a newly opened bottle, I took it from her and tried to ape Riesling's stunt. But for the life of me I couldn't swallow in consecutive gulps more than about a third of the contents. The critic really was a remarkable talent.

As I drank, Hinkle identified the rest of the authors and their genres. As it happened, only Blond women wrote fiction, and according to him it was all obscene.

"Explicit hardcore sex, eh?"

He snorted indignantly. "There's no normal, decent crotchwork, if that's what you mean. This is real *filth*. The heroine is saved from some peril by the big, handsome, and wealthy nobleman, who then asks for her hand in marriage. The one I read made me puke my guts out. I wouldn't want one to get into the hands of any daughter of mine, I tell you."

When he had finished, I asked, "Are there many Sebastianers who read books? If so, where do they get them? Not at the library."

"Various places," Hinkle said. "Whichever would be appropriate to the theme of the particular book. My own, for example, are distributed where children congregate: playgrounds, birthday parties, and so on. Hozenblatt's tomes, being so heavy, are stacked in gyms used by weight lifters. The female porn is made available at hairdressing salons."

"And Riesling's criticism?" The large, jovial man fascinated me. It looked as though he seized life and made it groan.

Hinkle shrugged. "The fact is, it's never been printed." He leaned closer to me. "Some say, never been written. None of the rest of us has ever seen it, I know that."

"Remarkable! But he seems happy enough, doesn't he? Is he telling us something?" I took another swallow of wine. "And does anybody do playwriting, which I raffishly call my own racket?"

"No one," said Hinkle.

"Then the art would be another good subject for Riesling!" I cried. I was feeling the wine now. I looked across at the critic. He had got Inga to bring him another enormous plate of food, great forkfuls of which he was shoveling into his open mouth. His eyes were closed in bliss.

"Hey, Riesling!" I shouted. He opened his watery eyes but continued to eat. "Catch!" I hurled the bottle at him. With horror I watched him do nothing whatever to seize or deflect it. It struck him squarely in the forehead and bounced off as if it, or his skull, were made of rubber. He closed his eyes again and went on eating.

I shouted his name once more, and then:

> "Shall I compare thee to a summer's day?
> Thou art more lovely, and more temperate . . ."

The critic immediately dropped his loaded fork, went to his armpit, and brought out a large automatic pistol. His first shot broke the glass in front and slightly to the right of me; the slug continued past my forearm with a hideous whistle.

I didn't wait for another. I plunged to the floor and left the room on running hands and feet. I hurled myself down the stairs and dashed out the door of the pink house and leaped into the waiting rickshaw, ordering Helmut to depart on the double.

But, looking back, I saw I was not pursued. The life of the Sebastiani authors, however intramurally passionate it was, never crossed the threshold to make contact with the great world. And no doubt that was best for the country.

Once we were beyond the Street of Words, I directed Helmut to pull over to the curb. Riesling's attack had returned me to sobriety. I realized that I should sit quietly somewhere and try to make some sense of what I'd seen and heard since arriving in Saint Sebastian. I might use Helmut as a sounding board. He was so stupid that I would not appear foolish no matter what nonsense I bounced off him; also, he had no personal axe to grind.

We were on a street of low wooden sheds, each separated from the next by some distance; no people were in view or in hearing.

"Here's how it looks to me," I said towards Helmut but really to myself. "The prince is a pervert, an eccentric, and so on, but as rulers go, he's far from being the worst imaginable, because he has no effect on the country."

"Sir vill vish—"

"Please, Helmut, I'm trying to follow a train of thought. You wouldn't understand, but I have been sent over here from my country to find out what happens in yours. If we like what we see, we will give you money."

"Is interesting place," Helmut said, pointing to the sheds. He picked up the shafts. "You should look."

"What is it?" I asked. "It resembles the fireworks factory that was at the edge of my hometown when I was a child."

"Yass," said Helmut, pulling me into a graveled lane that went amongst the little frame buildings.

"You mean it *is* a fireworks factory?"

The establishment of my childhood had been surrounded by a high fence topped with barbed wire and everywhere posted with warnings as to the explosive nature of what was made therein and the danger of fire. Here there was nothing to restrain the layman or -child from wandering about the premises, not even an informational sign.

Helmut stopped before a certain hut, which was distinguished in no way from its fellows, lowered the shafts, and went to the door of weathered wood, saying "Come, please," and I did as asked.

Inside, along three of the four walls, were workbenches at each of which sat a middle-aged woman. The one nearest me, her gray-blond hair in a bun, was pouring what would seem to be gunpowder through a funnel into a stout red cardboard tube. She did this none too carefully, for a dusting of the black powder covered the tabletop.

"Very interesting," I told Helmut, and turned nervously away. "I really must get back to the hotel."

Ignoring me, he went to the center of the room and pushed aside the rough-woven rug that lay there, uncovering a trapdoor. He bent and grasped the recessed ring that was its handle and pulled up the door, revealing a wooden ladder that descended to some space below. He beckoned me to follow and went first. Curiosity overcame my apprehensions. There was an earthen smell at the bottom of the ladder and no light whatever for a moment; then Helmut produced an electric torch from somewhere. He led me through a low, narrow tunnel whose ceiling and sides were braced with timbers. Just as it occurred to me that I should probably worry about being asphyxiated, we turned a corner, went through a crude door that resembled the end of a packing crate, and entered a chamber lighted by several kerosene lamps atop a coarse wooden table and, I was relieved to see, ventilated by a vertical pipe going up through the ground above. Nevertheless it was not the kind of retreat that would have appealed to the claustrophobe.

Camp chairs were arranged around the table, and Helmut, with a new authority and in a new accent, asked me to choose one and take a seat.

He stood before me. "Olga will be coming along in a few moments," he said. "Along with the rest of the Revolutionary Council. We haven't been able to get together with you until now, because each of us has a demanding, and of course degrading, job he or she must perform for at least ten hours a day or night. It is not generally known, I think, that one of the major problems in making a revolution is merely scheduling the conspiratorial meetings—if the persons involved are flunkies in their society."

Temporarily dumbstruck by the transformation, I sank onto one of the chairs and stared at the hard-packed earth between my feet.

At last I looked up. "You're telling me that *you* and your sister are leaders of the Sebastiani liberation movement?"

Helmut sneered. "The belief that we all look alike is but another manifestation of the bias against us. We are siblings only in the ideological and not the biological sense."

This was a familiar plaint of oppressed minorities, and, so far as I was concerned, usually justifiable enough. On the other hand, *these* people had blown up my home. I reminded Helmut of that outrage.

He moved his square chin. "A man posing as an agent for the owner of the building assured us it was not only unoccupied but scheduled to be demolished."

"The individual in reference was undoubtedly that swine who does janitorial work around the place," said I.

Helmut's nostrils flared. "In Saint Sebastian he would be a Blond."

"No doubt," I said. "But I hasten to assure you that such a chap in New York City is a social pariah only by reason of his own personality, not because of before-the-fact prejudice. I've seldom seen a black super in a white building. Finally, an Afro-American friend of mine, with a Harlem super of his own kind, had the same complaints as I. Along with one that remained unique: *his* super used a passkey to slip into the apartment and eat all the fresh fruit."

Helmut shrugged. "If you remember, you did get a telephone warning as soon as it was discovered that you were on the premises. We had no motive to wish you harm."

But I did not hear him offer to compensate me for the loss of property. He displayed the solipsist self-righteousness that has always kept me from wholeheartedly admiring the ideologue even when I give general assent to his proximate aim.

At that moment a woman came in from the tunnel. She was tall and full-figured, wore rumpled dark slacks and a shapeless gray coat; her hair was gathered within a beret, and she wore spectacles.

I assumed she was a hitherto-unencountered member of the Revolutionary Council—until she seized my hand, yanked it up and pushed it down, and said, "Good day, Brother Wren. We meet in other conditions than yesterday's."

I leaned forward and squinted. "Olga? Can it be?"

She laughed coldly. "Is that not a vile role I must play?" Then in came several other men and women, all of whom were fair-complexioned. They sat down on the camp chairs, but Olga remained standing.

"We'll make this brief," said she. "Rudy and Margit and some of you others are supposed to be on duty right now. Fortunately, the conviction that we all look alike helps us at such a time. *They* never quite know who's who." She directed the last comment to me.

I was still trying to habituate myself to the new Olga, who was even more remarkable than the new Helmut.

She continued. "Brother Wren, as some of us know already,

has been sent over by the US government to determine how best to aid our movement."

At this point I recovered sufficiently to interrupt. "Excuse me," I said, "but that's not quite the case." The Blonds all turned and gave me uncompromising stares. In the modest refulgence of the kerosene lamps their eyes were darker than the normal sky blue. They were all rather large people. I quickly edited my statement. "That is, it might be premature to put it as you have. Anyway, I am a humble information-gatherer, not a policy-maker."

Olga resumed as if I had not spoken. "We want arms that are light and portable: automatic rifles, machine pistols. We don't need planes. Sebastian doesn't have an air force, and he doesn't have any armor, so we don't need tanks. I suppose if we had artillery we could shell the palace, but then we'd have to go to the expense of rebuilding it, for we will want to maintain a commanding structure up there for the executive offices of the democratic government to come. It's the highest point in the city and figures too importantly in the ruling symbolism of our country to dispense with."

She was an impressive figure, standing there before us, though her clothes were drab. I do not ritualistically gasp in admiration at the sterner sort of woman (who has always, beginning with my grade-school gym teacher, an iron-jawed bruiser named Bertha Dirkwalter, tended to be impatient with me), but I had to admit that Olga was morally more prepossessing now than when posing as an airborne airhead.

She went on. "Annaliese, Hans, and I, as the Subcommittee on Arms, have drawn up a list of the weaponry we require from America." She nodded at one of the other women, attired and spectacled as soberly as herself but underneath it all, one could discern, another Valkyrie only slightly less handsome than her leader. "Please give Brother Wren that list."

Annaliese opened her blouse, reached within, and brought out a sheaf of papers, which she handed across to me. They were warm from contact with her flesh, which, judging from the set of her shoulders, was ample.

"I'll look these over," I said, placing the papers on the table. "But again I must remind you that somebody with more authority than I will make the judgment as to any aid, military or otherwise."

"Of course, we will require a good deal more than arms," Olga said, as usual making no acknowledgment of my reservations. "We'll need one hundred million dollars to begin with. I won't waste our time with a list of specific allocations: we're quite capable of making the dispersals ourselves. If you must justify it to your people, tell them the largest single outlay will consist of bribes to those around Sebastian. His advisors and ministers are so corrupt that we might well bring him down bloodlessly: that should appeal to you Americans."

"In which case you wouldn't need the arms," I pointed out.

Olga's fair face darkened. "I'm afraid that, on the contrary, weapons must always, if deplorably, have the highest priority. For it is likely that as soon as Sebastian is removed, our neighbors will see what they will interpret as our time of weakness in which they might strike with success."

The other Blonds murmured their fervent agreement with this analysis, and Annaliese smote the tabletop with her fist.

Intermittently I was still having seizures of astonishment at the change in Olga.

I said, "As I think you have reason to know, I was transported to Saint Sebastian in a comatose state and had not been well briefed beforehand. I'm not sure I can remember your abutting neighbors. Austria? Czechoslovakia, one or both Germanies?"

Olga proceeded to pronounce names which, never having heard them before or seen them written, I can reproduce only approximately. "Gezieferland on the north, and to the southeast, Swatina."

"My ignorance of these countries is absolute. I take it they are as small as Saint Sebastian? What sort of regimes do they have?"

"Tyrannical," said she. "One is ruled by a king and the other, a grand duke, two scoundrels who are in fact cousins to Sebastian."

"Why would they be eager to attack this country?"

"They have no Blonds of their own," said Olga.

"They would like to enslave you for their own purposes?"

"Need you ask?" She made a gesture of impatience. "It's time for our people to get back to their jobs before they're missed.

And I'm sure you are eager to get to the cable office to contact your principals with our demands."

I winced. "Just a moment. You're speaking of demands now? Or was that a slip of the tongue?"

Olga said coldly, "Not at all, Brother Wren. I'm afraid we must hold you hostage until we receive an affirmative response from your government."

6

THERE WAS LITTLE QUESTION that I could be easily restrained by the large Blond men, and therefore I attempted no physical resistance.

But I could say, "I find your tactics leave something to be desired. Remember, I am first the man whose home you destroyed, along with the script of a play that might have been produced on Broadway, making me rich and famous. Then I am literally kidnaped by an agency of the US government, drugged, and sent over here. As if that isn't enough, you now inform me that I am to be used as a pawn in your game. You certainly know how to attract sympathizers."

Oblivious to my remarks, the Blonds rose from the table. Helmut remained at the door; the others left.

"There's nothing personal in it," said Olga. "You should not take offense. The individual cannot be respected in such an effort as ours, else nothing would be accomplished. Our country is already badly behind the times. Who else in the world is governed by such a degenerate as Sebastian?"

"Ironically enough, some of the newest nations in the so-called Third World might provide a rival or two," said I. "But even if I agreed that you Blonds are in a peculiarly subservient situation in Europe, even if you might require brute force to depose the prince, why must you work your will by violent means on foreigners, strangers who have no proper involvement in your affairs?"

A sneer hardened the shape of Olga's full mouth. "Do you think anyone would even hear of us, let alone care, if we were nonviolent? You have just admitted you are here only as result of our bombing your home. Then we were successful! Why should we be concerned with your inconvenience, even your pain? Did you care about ours?" She sighed in impatience. "Wren, the humanistic platitudes belong in the schoolbooks. They have no meaning in the real world."

This argument, like all the effective ones in my experience of life, was not original, but except in the hands of geniuses, innovation tends to be little more than thrillseeking. In any event, I had virtually exhausted, for the moment, my capacity for debate on the subject at hand: Aristotle to the contrary notwithstanding, I am not to any degree a political animal: I just wish people would be quietly nice and fair to one another and there would never be any riots, revolutions, wars. I am aware that hope is weak-minded, but I am confident that it is normal amongst the rank and file of all nations, creeds, and breeds.

Helmut was still there. No doubt he was to be my private guard, and so far as I was concerned, husky as he was, he would be sufficient even though unarmed. Were he as stupid as I had originally believed, I would have assumed I could easily outwit him. As it was, I seemed to be a prisoner.

Imagine then my pleased surprise when Olga spoke to her comrade in a strange tongue, and he nodded (rather sullenly, I thought) and exited into the tunnel. I reproduce her speech as well as I can; I never saw written Sebastiani.

"*Helmut, alley yets. Idge lee manazhay.*"

I intended to wait until he had had time to reach the surface, and then to overpower Olga by the most expeditious means, using as much force as was needed: despite the current trends, I dislike using violence against women, but this was not the moment for the gentlemanly restraint shown by the heroes of World War II films, who are unable to punch even a female Nazi.

To kill time, I asked her about the local language: who spoke it, when, and why?

"What you just said to Helmut was at the threshold of intelligibility for me. It seemed some combination of several modern European tongues."

Olga was staring at me, a new emotion behind the lenses of

her severe spectacles. She said, "You are not altogether unattractive."

"Uh, thank you, Olga. Neither are you. In fact, you're beautiful, even as you're dressed right now, which I gather is supposed to be antiseptic."

"You don't have one of those New York diseases, do you?"

"Pardon?"

"Herpes or that peculiarly virulent new strain of gonorrhea?"

"Good heavens, no!"

"Then I want to screw." She began to remove her clothing. "This may not be impeccable revolutionary practice, because you really must get off that cable without delay, but I have normal sexual appetites, and who knows when such a moment will come again?" Her long skirt was already off and hanging over one of the chairs. I noted for what it was worth that irrespective of her outer attire, the overabundance of the revolutionary's garb or the brevity of the stewardess's uniform, underwear was unknown to Olga.

I was about to protest in the name of my natural modesty when it occurred to me that such a moment as this would beautifully suit my intention to escape. In another instant Olga would be starkers, whereas I had not yet even pretended to begin to undress, a lack of preparedness which she had not yet, in her egocentricity, noticed.

But the fact was that when Olga had stripped to the altogether, she was not as easy to leave as I had anticipated. Indeed, in a sexual career of some dimension, I had not seen the like of her body, for which "magnificent" would have been an inadequate term. I began, all but involuntarily, to remove my own clothes. . . . Having no intention of catering to those who hold a book in one hand, I omit the details of the succeeding moments, except to say that Olga proved to be even more of a handful than she looked: I might even go so far as to say that her performance led me to question whether I had ever previously had any encounter which could be called carnal.

I was not aware of how much this experience had taken out of me until I heard a snapping of fingers and an impatient voice saying, "Come along, Wren. The Revolution can't wait while you snooze," and opened my eyes and saw that Olga was all dressed while I still lay on the tabletop, feeling as though I were a half-melted stick of butter. It was chagrining to me to remember that not so long before I had been planning to jump her while I was dressed and she was naked!

I creakily climbed down and retrieved the clothes I had dropped on the floor. Bending my back was an exercise in anguish.

"Let's go," she nagged.

"You're stronger than you think," I wincingly murmured as I secured my belt, which now could be cinched one hole further on the skinny side.

However, once I was attired, I reflected that we were on terra firma now, and not in the horizontal situation in which she had a natural advantage (please, no feminist outcries: whoever *contains* another is perforce boss!). She was big and strong, but I was wiry and had studied the martial arts for at least four sessions with an Oriental whose dojo shared the second floor of a ramshackle Garment District building with a bathhouse staffed by his female countrymen, adepts in that art of pressure-point massage called *shiatsu*, which is not obscene (I should say, not *necessarily* obscene) and had the polka-dotted belt to prove it.

I assumed the fighting stance taught me (not sans pain) by my slant-eyed *sensei*, and said, "I'm not going to be kept your prisoner, Olga, but I will promise, after only a little more investigation—for frankly I'm eager to get home—to return to the USA and make a thorough report to my superiors on Saint Sebastian. Be assured that your argument will be well represented, if you'll answer only a few questions. First, if you Blonds are as clever as you obviously are when you drop your masks of subservience, why have you taken so long to make your move? So far as I can see, the prince does little to enforce his will on the populace. Such power as he possesses seems to be used exclusively for self-protection. The security measures at the palace would bring bliss to a paranoiac. I have not encountered any soldiers or any policemen but a couple of low-comedy municipal constables. So who enforces the tyranny of which you complain?"

Olga's face had taken on a very bland, very blond mien. "And what else would you like to know?"

"Well, what's puzzling me is, I haven't yet met many examples nor have I seen much evidence of a Sebastiani middle class. In America, even in New York, most of the people you see at any given time, unless you constantly frequent the venues of the lumpenproletariat or the watering places of the plutocrats, are those in the middle: they work at something during the day and come home at night; they are usually married and probably have offspring; it is they who give the plurality to whichever presidential candidate, after he and his rivals have so strenuously curried their favor. The news is published and/or broadcast for them. Most kinds of entertainment are offered with them in mind, and cars, refrigerators, and home computers are designed to meet their existing needs or create new ones. This kind of people has been conspicuous by its absence thus far in my Sebastiani experience. I've seen a few jeering urchins; a clutch of scholars, a gaggle of authors; some hotel personnel, *et al.*, and most recently, a band of revolutionaries. But where are the ordinary folks, the regulars, the normal population, the crowd, the mob, the herd, elevated over the centuries of growing enlightenment in the Western countries, from Spenser's 'rascal many' to 'the people' of the social reformers, and finally, at least in the US, to the sort of human beings who fill the stands at the Super Bowl—which as you undoubtedly know, flying to the States as you do so often, is the major public event of any year in my country."

Exhausted by speaking so long while standing in the karate position, thighs at right angles to my calves, fists at the ready, I straightened up to receive Olga's answer. But as soon as I was off guard she kneed me in the stomach and, as I buckled, struck me with a right cross that would have felled any of the current contenders. I blacked out as I fell, but came to not long after meeting the floor.

Olga stooped, lifted me to her back, and with the fireman's carry transported me along the tunnel to the overhead trapdoor. Riding comfortably along on her back, I expected her to carry me up the ladder with the same ease in which she had negotiated the tunnel, but my awakening was rude. She put me on my feet, back against the ladder, and continued to slap my face long after it should have been obvious I had regained consciousness.

"Will you stop?" I cried, fending off her hands. "And don't

attack me again! I subscribe to an ancient moral code by which a man cannot strike a woman. I tell you it was a better world when that was in force." I woozily, sorely climbed the ladder to the room where the women were making giant firecrackers. No doubt it was from this source that the makings had come for the bomb that destroyed my home.

Olga emerged and then closed the trapdoor behind her.

"Wasn't it careless to have left that open all this while?" I asked.

"No. They would never come in here. They're scared of the gunpowder." She hooked her arm through mine. "We're going to the cable office now. Don't try to escape unless you want to be permanently crippled."

She had been an animal when undressed. I still felt half lame. I was disinclined to test my strength against hers once more. Beyond this consideration, it was not unpleasant to be so closely clutched by such a woman as she: her right breast rubbed my left biceps at each step, and occasionally I was brushed by the arch of her Lachaise hip. Hers was the most generous body with which I had ever been intimate. I believed it unfortunate that she was so obsessively political.

We walked through the town. I cannot explain why our route was more or less flat when the rickshaw ride had been as if on a roller coaster, unless it was that Helmut had taken a circuitous and undulating journey for the purpose of flexing his muscles.

I tried again to talk to Olga. "I wish you would give me some explanation as to why you Blonds are in the existing situation. You are all splendid physical specimens of humanity, and I suspect that the members of the Revolutionary Council are not the only intelligent members of your breed. How is it, then, that you are servants to those whose masters you should be? Are you aware that only a half-century ago a dictator named Hitler, in a country not too far from here, made your type his ideal?"

At last I had said something that provoked a response from her. "And was not Hitler himself dark-haired, sallow-skinned, narrow-shouldered, and pudgy-bellied? And were any of his close associates blond or, for that matter, even physically fit?"

"But is it your implication that attractive, healthy, fair-complexioned persons are at natural disadvantage in Europe or, for that matter, the human race? I don't think that blonds are losers in Scandinavia, or in American show business."

But Olga had returned to silence. Perhaps she was the woman-of-action type, to whom matters of rationale were boring. I'll admit that despite my job (which I always think of as temporary), I tend to look for a theoretical place in which to file each phenomenon. We made an odd but complementary couple.

Had the pace she set not been so demanding, I might have enjoyed the walk more as we passed a series of colorful open-air markets. At the largest of these, all manner of food was for sale, great wheels of golden-fleshed, red-rinded cheese, plump artichokes, sleek aubergines, striped melons, blushing pears, wicker-encased demijohns of ruby-red wine, jugs of foaming cider, and eviscerated pheasants, woodcock, and hares, suspended from boothfront hooks. The food stalls were attended by outsized women, with great thick red arms and strong, raucous voices, in which they exchanged abuse and cried the virtues of their wares, which included generous displays of the fruits of the sea (though so far as I knew, Saint Sebastian was nowhere near saltwater): bins of corrugated green oysters, blue-black mussels, the little marine hedgehogs called sea urchins, living langoustes and crayfish, huge crosscuts of tuna, tiny prawns, tentacular squid . . .

In a contiguous square was a riotously multicolored flower market. Here the vendors were winsome girls in the years of pubescence, their faces fresh as the blossoms they sold. Then on into an entire street lined on either curbing with birdcages, tended by short black-haired men of cheery mien, who exchanged whistles, chirps, squeaks, with the fowl that were their wares: minuscule finches, high-crested cockatoos, peevish-eyed parrots, a laughing magpie, and warbling canaries.

But one conspicuous lack distinguished each of the markets from those elsewhere in the world: no customers were in evidence!

"There you are," I said to Olga. "Who buys the goods offered for sale by these merchants? Again I ask, where is the *public?*"

By now we were turning into the familiar street in which the Hotel Bristol was situated. We had passed no fellow pedestrians during a twenty-minute walk, and no vehicle had used any of the nearby roads.

Olga's response was to nod towards the hotel and jerk my arm. "There'll be time enough to send the cable. I'm feeling lustful again. You're not as sexually ineffectual as I supposed, though probably part of your allure for me is simply that you have dark hair and are puny."

I overlooked the slur in my amazement at her appetites. Perhaps she had revealed her exploitable weakness. After the workout she had given me in the underground room, such legendary satyrs as Victor Hugo and John Paul Jones would have needed time for recuperation, and therefore it was not likely that I would be capable of soon again being distracted from an intention to escape.

So I showed a burst of false enthusiasm, brought her arm more tightly against my side (where a rib was still sore from the pressure of her steel thighs), and insofar as it was ever possible with Olga, pretended to take the initiative in a vigorous stride into the hotel.

When the concierge saw Olga his face contorted in revulsion, and he said to me, "Blonds are not permitted to enter the hotel except in the role of a servant."

I was caught by surprise, but Olga said immediately, "I am nurse." She reached into one of the capacious pockets of her coat and produced a small purse, which in turn yielded a document encased in glassine. "Is license." She showed this to the concierge, who waved it away in disgusted assent. Yet Olga found it needful to go further. "Will give enema," said she. "He has tourist constipation." No doubt it could have been predicted that in Saint Sebastian the complaint suffered by visitors to other countries would be reversed.

No sooner had the elevator doors closed on us than Olga seized and opened my belt buckle and pulled my trousers to my ankles. I defended my drawers, but with two quick hands at the elastic in back, she was rapidly baring my fundament. The last-named was pressed against the rear wall of the car, and it could anyway not answer her needs, so soon she abandoned that phase of the assault and went again to my groin, this time with a combination of feint and brute power, and succeeded in exposing it just as we reached our destination, the fourth floor, and the door opened on Clyde McCoy.

"I see it hasn't taken you any time at all to go bad in a permissive society," said he with a dirty smirk.

Olga pulled me off the elevator and in the hallway continued to try to undress me as though we were alone and behind a closed door. She was utterly devoid of shame. I suppose it was the presence of my alcoholic countryman that gave me the strength to hold my own against her for a few moments, and then, when the tide was turning back in her favor, to knock her out with a punch to the jaw that almost broke my knuckles.

McCoy had stayed in the hall to watch the ruckus, and when Olga was down he gave me a hand of applause. I pulled up and secured my clothing, and was immediately contrite: I knelt and examined my opponent for serious damage. I found none. She breathed regularly.

McCoy jeered. "Don't worry, a Blond has an iron jaw and a granite head. I should have known you were an SM man."

"Put a sock in it, McCoy, and give me some help. How can I keep this woman from molesting me without having her actually arrested or really hurting her?"

Wryly he shook his head. "How to get somebody to do something they hate and still have them love you. That's a Yank for you! But over here that kinda shit don't go. Want somebody off your back, you drop 'em."

"Come on, be serious. I've got a problem." Despite Olga's ruthless using of me for her own purposes, sexual and political, my basic sympathies were still weighted towards her cause.

"I'm telling you," said McCoy. "You don't have to put up with anything from a Blond. You can throw her out the window."

"I'm afraid I don't subscribe to the Sebastiani code, and I must say I am appalled to know that you do. Even though you've lived here for years, you still call yourself an American."

"Pigshit," McCoy growled. "Did you not ask my help?"

"I regret that," I said frostily. Olga made a sound. She was becoming conscious. I had to slug her again or flee. I really do hate to hit a girl, especially one with whom I have recently had intimate congress—though now that I think about it, would an utter stranger be more appropriate?

I fled. I ran down the hall and around the corner and into a veritable wall consisting of the large body of the man who listened to the recorded voice of Enrico Caruso while bathing. He was about to let himself into what I assumed to be his room.

"*Per favore, signore,*" I pleaded, exhausting my store of ready Italian, "can you give me refuge? I'll explain this as soon as I can."

He performed a (given his figure) necessarily generous shrug and gestured, with a rolled-out palm, for me to proceed him into the room. Then he swept in behind me and closed the door before Olga had reached that section of the hall, though I could hear her running footfalls. With another similar gesture he indicated I should take a seat on the sofa, a decent-looking piece of furniture upholstered in flowered brocade. We were in a comfortable sitting room. My Mediterranean friend appeared to have a suite for himself. One of the several doors undoubtedly led to a bedroom, and another set, louvered, he now opened to reveal a neat little kitchenette of the type I once enjoyed in Manhattan (if you can say that about a combined roach resort and mouse spa in which the fridge was on permanent defrost whatever the adjustment and only half a burner worked on the quarter-sized stove).

The large man had been carrying, somewhere beneath my line of sight, which was focused first on his huge hairy face and now on his massive middle body, a string bag full of groceries. This he now placed in the little sink and began to empty. There were several elongated boxes of the size in which spaghetti was packed, a handful of greenery, a great wedge of cheese, and some other surely edible items.

Next he brought me a tumbler full of red wine, carrying in his other large hand a raffia-wrapped vessel of gallon capacity. With an amiable display of very white teeth, he pantomimed Bottom's Up, then went back to the kitchenette I could hardly see when he stood before it.

I thought I should wait a while before speaking, lest Olga be listening at doors, and therefore I drank my wine in silence. The big fellow refilled the glass occasionally without my asking, but his principal effort was applied to cooking spaghetti in a giant-sized pot and grinding, with mortar and pestle, enough garlic to scent the room, and then what from the bouquet I could identify as basil (having had, a few years previously, an affair with a married woman who would rather cook for me than go to bed: her husband was OK at sex but a slob when it came to cuisine, said she, "with this food revolution exploding all around us").

By the time my friend served up the *pesto genovese*, on a side table which became dining-sized by the elevation of two hinged panels, I was a bit pissed from having gulped the wine into a stomach lately agitated by my passionate encounter with Olga. He had given each of us a mound of greenflecked spaghetti that rose from tabletop to eye-level, and now, before I could so much as approach my portion with a weary hand, he had reduced his own by half, in the consuming of which he lowered his head, tucked the fork into the side of the heap, and shoveled violently while his lips produced a suction that a Hoover might have envied.

I finally wound a few strands onto my fork and ingested them: very tasty. I took another slug of red.

"I haven't been over here for long," I said, "but I've already been exposed to a number of Sebastiani phenomena, and thus far what I've learned seems to cancel itself out in every respect. The prince is in theory a tyrant from a much earlier epoch, but in practice he is apparently harmless. He does nothing but eat rich food. His sexual tastes are pederastic. None of his subjects can be in want, for they enjoy unlimited credit.

"Now the Blonds may be second-class citizens and condemned to the menial work, waiting on tables, pulling rickshaws, and so on, but according to the prince they also practice law and certain other professions that are more or less honorific elsewhere. Their women are obliged to have sexual relations with anyone who asks them, but the only Blond female with whom I am acquainted virtually raped *me*, so one might question how onerous they consider the obligation, for I was all but a stranger to her. And it should be noted that the Blonds are splendid physical specimens, tall and strong and comely, unlike any other oppressed people on record."

During my remarks the large man nodded frequently but continued to gorge on pesto, refilling his own plate and raising his heavy eyebrows when he looked at mine, still loaded from the first serving. To be polite I gobbled up a few lengths and washed them down with another flood of wine, which I saw was, according to the label, a local estate-bottled vintage of something called Valpolifella *(sic)* and could be characterized as being red and wet.

I resumed. "The scholars of Saint Sebastian are lazy buffoons, and the male writers are a pack of swine. Incidentally, the pornography is allegedly written only by Blond females, but I haven't checked this out for myself, and I must say I wouldn't place much credence in the unsupported word of any of the scribblers I have met. On the other hand, again I can't see that much actual harm is done by any of these gentry, for only a few people read, and according to the official librarian, himself an illiterate, what each reads is the same book, over and over again.

"The law-enforcement procedure is ridiculous. People are punished harshly for rudeness, but on the other hand, anybody can accuse anyone else of any crime and be believed by the police."

My host raised a full tumbler of wine and poured it down his throat with the sound of a flushing toilet. He smacked his lips and rose to carry his empty plate to the spaghetti pot, which had remained on the stove, looked within, and finding nothing left, sighed massively and went to the wardrobe, where he removed the jacket and vest of the black serge suit he wore, but retained his white shirt and dark necktie. He put on a maroon silk dressing gown and tied its tasseled belt around his tremendous midsection. After politely bowing to me, he loosened his collar, strapped across his eyes the black sleep-mask he took from a pocket in the robe, and lay down upon the bed, which sagged until its mattress-springs almost touched the floor.

Obviously it was time to terminate my exterior monologue. I had got some profit from drawing up the oral bill of particulars with respect to the country I found myself in. I had confirmed my suspicion that Saint Sebastian was an unusually difficult place about which to generalize. No doubt this was true of every society: e.g., how to characterize a city shared at once by the South Bronx junkie, the gilded tenant of Trump Tower, the cop from Queens, and the Broadway headliner? But I had yet to see a significant relation between any two of the Sebastiani milieus, including the court and the Blonds, each of which would seem to have only a theoretical reality for the other. And I thought I could remember from my college reading of history that it is never the oppressed people which make a revolution, but rather the class between the rulers and those at the bottom: *viz.*, the very class which was not in evidence in any large numbers in Saint Sebastian . . . but then, human beings of any kind were in short supply, owing to the current contrast to the clamorous Manhattan throng amidst which I normally pursued my destiny. On my first day in the capital city I had seen, all told, not as many mortals as one would encounter in a midday walk from my old loft to Rothman's delicatessen.

Rothman's Deli! Never when it was accessible did I dream that one day in a far-off land a mental reference to it would move me to nostalgia. Given the difference in time, back home it would be morning now, and the customers would be coming in for their fresh bagels and bialys, milk-blue coffee in bone-white containers, and sweating prune Danish. The street criminals would have wiped the gore from their switchblades, put their Saturday Night Specials on safety, and slunk, or more likely swaggered, to their lairs for a well-earned rest. The tarts were in bed at last to sleep, and the derelicts had not yet risen from their doorways. Here and there a leashed dog would be enjoying his matutinal bowel movement; a few would even be doing it legally, below the curb. The vehicular traffic would not yet have begun to accelerate towards the homicidal mania of noon. Perhaps the odd cabdriver would suggest, with spasmodic gestures and abrupt sounds, the hysteria that would claim him absolutely later in the day, but seen so early the display might be taken for harmless, even charming verve. And at this hour the sidewalk pedestrian undoubtedly ran the least risk all day of being called "motherfucker" by another human being who was an utter stranger to him.

In short, I was astonished to discover that I missed New York, perhaps not to the degree that I was ready to sing that fatuous song rendered, at the behest of the Tourist Bureau, by show-biz celebs who love Gotham so ardently as to reside in California, but I did identify in myself a homesickness, if it could be so termed, for the quotidian life of Manhattan as opposed to what I had thus far encountered over here, where everything was so *foreign.* Could I have been turning into what, as a man of culture, I had, my adult life long, despised: *viz.*, the provincial xenophobe?

I pushed away the now cold pesto, went to the door, opened it a crack, and took the lie of the land. It would have been less kind to awaken the enormous man from his nap, I thought, than to leave quietly without tendering my thanks. I had decided to repair to the cable office, if I could elude Olga, and send a message to Rasmussen demanding that he withdraw me from this country where I could not be protected from its capricious nationals. . . . No, such a negative appeal would never succeed with a sadistic superior. I had it: I would rather employ some such strategy as more than one grim wit had suggested "we" should have done in Vietnam: i.e., simply declare victory and leave. I would assure Rasmussen I had seen enough to write an authoritative report on Saint Sebastian, and suggest what American policy should be towards the little principality: neglect, and rather more indifferent than benign.

7

"AH," SAID THE CONCIERGE as I passed through the lobby, "I do hope you are now eliminating your stools painlessly, my dear sir, and will not again require the services of your Blond colonic irrigationist."

"By the way," I replied, "did you see her leave?"

"I have not," said he. "But I'm sure she has done so if she's not with you. She would certainly know the consequences if found in the hotel without authorization."

"Would you mind telling me what those consequences would be?"

He frowned and then said, "I really haven't the slightest idea. It's the sort of thing one says."

"Much of Sebastiani existence consists in such statements, does it not? You people speak on the extravagant side, but so far as I can see, the reality is much tamer."

He looked crestfallen. I hastened to say, "I'm not criticizing, mind you! It's certainly preferable to a state of affairs in which violence is commonplace, as it is where I come from, where furthermore it's fashionable in certain milieus to pretend that at any given time the situation is all that it should be." Already I was less homesick. "I once lived in an apartment building every tenant of which was robbed at gunpoint, in the lobby, by a band of neighborhood thugs who were contestants in an all-city mugging competition. When our hooligans lost to the Kip's Bay team, the victims were indignant and gave the criminals a consolation party."

"Well, then," he said bitterly, "isn't everything always more colorful in New York?"

I had perhaps gone too far and hurt his feelings. "I wonder whether you get my meaning?" I asked. "I'm flattering you, by contrast."

His greasy smile instantly reappeared. "I understand perfectly. Now would you like a boy?"

"No, thank you, and kindly never ask me that question again. What you might do however is tell me why I see so few people wherever I go in Saint Sebastian? And most of those people I do encounter are working at some kind of job that serves the public. But no public is in evidence." I specified the open-air markets.

He thought for a moment, the tip of a finger at his pursed lips. "I have it! Those who sell fruit buy pets from the bird people, who in turn purchase cheese, and so on." He wore a self-congratulatory expression, which I did not wish to darken by expressing dubiety.

I left the hotel. Unless Olga was still looking for me in the hallways upstairs, she had made an exit unobserved by the concierge and might attempt to waylay me in the street. I hugged the walls of the building on the short route to the cable office and saw neither her nor anyone else.

The bespectacled clerk was at the counter when I entered the office.

I obtained a cable form from him, as well as the stub of a pencil, unpleasantly marked as if by gnawing. The feckless Rasmussen had not provided me with a code in which to communicate with him. True, what I had to say was hardly the information that men would kill to get, but to be plainspoken in this context would seem unprofessional and might, if discovered, be used by the Firm's congressional critics as a pretext for appropriation-cutting.

The message I came up with was crafted from bygone slang of the 1930's and '40's, which would be instantly intelligible to any Yank however young, owing to nostalgia-film programs, but would surely be nonsensical language to one who had learned his English abroad.

SCREWBALLS VS. GOOFS. WOULD
NIX MOOLAH FOR ALL. UNCLE

DUDLEY FEELS LIKE SAP, WANTS
TO TAKE POWDER.

I handed the form to the clerk. "Please send this literally, letter by letter. Don't worry if it doesn't seem to say anything understandable to you, even if you think you're fluent in English."

He took it and held it high, in two hands, for a perusal. When he was done he winced and shook his head. "I'd think the Firm might have come up with a better code than this."

"What do you know about it?" I asked hotly. "That's impenetrable, if I do say so myself."

"I'm afraid no one else would," said he. "It's pathetically pellucid. You dismiss them all as eccentrics and wouldn't give money to any of them. You feel like a fool and want to go home."

I scowled at him. "Are you another ex-GI who was stranded here when the war ended?"

"I'm too young for that. But I have seen many of your motion pictures, including the excellent Boston Blackie films starring Chester Morris. Also those of Mary Beth Hughes, Jane Frazee, Vera Hruba Ralston—"

"Just a moment," I said, narrowing my eyes. "What do you take me for? You're making up those names. I'm a native American filmgoer, yet I've never heard of these people."

"So much the worse for you," said the clerk. "May I suggest you visit one of our cinemas during your stay in Saint Sebastian and acquire an education in your own movies. We have the very latest. Showing at the moment is the latest in the series about Rosie the Riveter. There's a new Western starring Johnny Mack Brown, and others with Charles Starrett, Bob Steele . . ."

These names being meaningless to me (I who, along with everyone else of a certain culture in New York, regard myself as a scholar of the films of Bogie, Bette, Coop, Hitch, *et al.)*, I asked, "Are you speaking in some kind of code?"

He sighed. "What can I say if the leading artists of your own country are unknown to you, except that frankly I am shocked. Those names are household words in Saint Sebastian, I assure you. Every child can recite them and more."

"But *are* there any children in this country?" I asked resentfully. "I've seen hardly any."

"Of course you haven't," said the clerk. "They're at the cinema all day."

I concluded that he was pulling my leg for certain. "And these moviehouses are everywhere, though I have yet to see a marquee?"

"Indeed they are," said he. "And they have no marquees. Public advertising of any kind, beyond the simple descriptive legend on a shop window, is illegal in Saint Sebastian. Everybody knows where the motion-picture houses are. There's one close by wherever you live, generally in the same street, and weekly schedules are sent to every household and of course posted in the outer lobbies of the cinemas." He smiled. "Oh yes, the movie theaters are in buildings which were formerly schools and churches."

"Aha." I was still far from sure he was not jesting. "That's why one sees so few people on the streets? They're all at the movies?"

"Except for those of us who are not so fortunate," said he, making a lantern jaw of self-pity. "I can't go until after business hours."

I leaned on the counter. "You're telling me that most of the population of this country, adults and children, spend most of their days at the movies?"

"Sure Mike!" he said with energy. "That's where all the bozos are, and the tomatoes and the small fry too. I don't mean maybe."

However reluctantly, I began to believe him. It was at any rate established that he was conversant in jargon that could have fooled me. I was embarrassed, and briefly considered, with a purpose to regain some ground, performing my Cagney imitation, but soon decided that that was all too routine even amongst native Americans who did not have the exotic cinematic lore at his command. I must be more ingenious to hold my own with this fellow. I decided I had no choice but to invent, to cut from the whole cloth, an actor who never existed, and to imitate him for the cable clerk.

"Tell me who this is." I screwed my mouth up, made one

eyelid sufficiently heavy to lower itself halfway, and spoke in a droning tone: "If you mugs think you can make a monkey outa me you got rocks inna head."

The clerk narrowed his eyes. "Just a minute. . . . That's not Barton MacLane? No, let me . . . Jack LaRue? No . . . Charles Bickford?"

"You'll be guessing all night," I told him triumphantly. "You see, I—"

"No, no, give me another chance! Did I hear a little bit of accent? Eduardo Ciannelli?"

"Believe me, you should give up," I said quickly. "It's an actor who made only a couple of low-budget pictures by comparison with which a Republic horse-opera was *Aïda.* Uh, his name was, uh, Ben Spinoza."

"Latin type?"

"You could say so."

The clerk snapped his fingers. "Yes, of course! He's playing in a film that just opened at the Linden Street cinema: *Gats 'n' Gals.*" He pouted. "I haven't been able to get there yet because of this damned job of mine."

I started to say, "That's imposs—" but decided it was really beneath me to keep this up. Instead I said coolly, "Please send this cable as soon as possible."

"To the Firm?"

I had yet to mention to whom it would be sent. Again I wondered whether this know-it-all was more than he seemed, but I decided against asking him, for whether or not he was, he would be certain to pretend to be—if that syntax will hold. Perhaps he had got that modus operandi from those old American movies, in which the heroes are invariably yea-sayers whose strides are jaunty, whose fedoras are cocked over one eye, and whose initially saucy girlfriends eventually go soft ("Aw, you big lug," etc.). But then I was thinking of the mainstream pictures: God knows what went on in the obscure B flicks so popular in Saint Sebastian.

"Yes, the Firm, Washington, DC."

"Isn't it rather Langley, VA?"

Again I was briefly suspicious, but on reflection I decided that McCoy had probably used the same channel of communication with the home office, a shockingly primitive one for an intelligence agency of a major world power, but no doubt that was just the point: the enemy would never look for such simplicity, which made impotent their computerized decoders. Anyway, it was a theory.

I sighed and told him to proceed. "Say, while I'm here: what's your position on the Blonds?"

"Aha. Well, personally I am incapable of bigotry. I think a fairhaired individual is quite as good as anybody else. I wouldn't want one for a friend, maybe, but—"

"Just a moment. You wouldn't?"

"A man has a right, has he not, to make the pals he chooses? I don't have the slightest interest in the culture of the Blonds. Why should I be forced to have an intimate who plays chess, a game I have never been able to understand; eats vegetables, which I loathe; and never has a cold, whereas the one I feel coming on at the moment will continue for months."

"Those are typical Blond tastes and traits?"

He grimaced. "They really are a pack of baboons. I say that without prejudice, of course. They are welcome to any advantages they can wrest from decent people."

"Do they have much of a resistance movement?"

He laughed and used another locution that must have derived from an old Hollywood production on a rube theme. "Gee whillikers, I wouldn't see any reason why. They're the happiest bunch you'll ever see, and why not. They don't do any work."

"They lie around and play the banjo?"

He frowned. "No. They play things like the cello and bassoon. Really dreary stuff. They're very boring people and much too lazy to want to change a social arrangement that suits them more than it does the rest of us." He looked at the cable form. "If you're going to leave us soon, you should make the most of your remaining time here."

"What would you suggest?"

He seized the pencil stub I had put back on the counter and put its end in his mouth, which explained the toothmarks on it. "Well, the Lido, if you like to swim. Longchamp, if you bet on the ponies. The Prater can be fun if you enjoy carousels. A cruise through the canals is a pleasant way to spend the afternoon. Picnicking in the Bois can be delightful, as is motoring to the nearby countryside to see the Summer Palace, the Greek amphitheater, or the great mosque erected during the Turkish Occupation, which is now the Museum of Quilts. Or may I suggest a visit to the Bourse. In the third cellar below the trading floor one can find Roman baths, their reservoirs and conduits still in working condition, their mosaics exquisite."

I said, with obvious irony, "Saint Sebastian is then a microcosm of Europe? Surely you have as well your own Versailles, Brandenburg Gate, and Erechtheum with a Caryatid Porch?"

He shrugged in satisfaction. "We are peculiarly blessed, I must admit. For that reason we Sebastianers are not great travelers."

"Also, on leaving the country one's overdraft and credit balance must be paid, no?"

"In fact that would be against the law."

"To leave the country?"

He shook his head. "No, no: to discharge one's debts *in toto.*"

"Can you be serious?"

The clerk spoke gravely. "It would be a profession of lack of faith in one's countrymen. No crime could be more heinous. Every Sebastianer has a God-given right to be owed money by others. Only in this way does he establish the moral pretext for running up his own large debts. Else our economy would collapse."

The dismal science has never been my strong suit. Whenever I've tried to understand how, in the same world, filled with the same people, buying and selling the same things, there can be regular periods of great prosperity, followed immediately by recessions, my brain spins on its axis (this would make sense only if the good times resulted from the purchase of Earth goods by visitors from Mars, who however on the next occasion took their business to Jupiter).

"If you say so," was my response. "But tell me: who makes these policies and/or laws? Not the prince?"

"Golly all get out," said the clerk, in an as usual without-warning resort to vintage-film idiom, "I think they must come down from the old days, most of them, but there is a legislative body that probably does something, though don't ask me what.

Oh, and there are some ministers. If you're interested in that sort of thing, you should stop at Government Square, just around the corner."

"All right, I shall." Ordinarily I'd walk a mile to elude the so-called social studies or those who practice them, but until officially relieved I was on a fact-finding mission—and I had no strong interest in seeing the derivative sights aforementioned (which suggested too strongly for me those scale models of the Taj Mahal, the Sphinx, the Eiffel Tower, and so on, constructed to lure tourists to otherwise colorless American backwaters). "Just tell me two more things. If the churches have been transformed into movie houses, what's become of the clergy? Yesterday I saw a man in priest's garb, riding a bicycle."

"They're now projectionists," he said enthusiastically.

"I suppose those at the top of the hierarchy, the bishops and so on, are film critics." I was joking only by half.

"Certainly not. That's illegal in Saint Sebastian! Anyone saying more than that he either liked or disliked a movie would be arrested and flogged."

I raised my brow. Now and again the ways of this country were not altogether foolish. "My last question concerns the language I heard some people speaking. In fact they were Blonds. What might that be?"

"It's some slang used only by Blonds. We call it Sebastard."

"It has ancient origins?"

"Naw," sneered the clerk. "They invented it so we wouldn't understand them when they spoke to one another in front of us. But who would want to know what a Blond was saying anyway?"

He gave me directions as to how to reach Government Square, and I left the cable office. The square proved to be that in which the concierge of my hotel had been pilloried, which I had seen when McCoy drove me back from the palace. The punitive device had another occupant today: shockingly, a boy who looked to be no more than nine or ten.

I stopped and spoke in commiseration. "You poor lad. What could you have done to deserve that?"

"Played hooky," said he in his voice of high pitch. "But I'm sick of Ken Maynard movies, and anyway I didn't want to sit in school all day in this nice weather. I wanted to go down to the river and mess around, fish or something." He had a saddle of freckles across his nose.

"I used to catch tadpoles when I was your age. I have degenerated since. You want me to let you out of this thing?" The gates of the pillory were secured with loose bolts that looked as if easy to dislodge.

He shook his head, on which the hair was cut high above the ears. "I could get out any time I want, these holes are so big." Wiggling his hands and feet, he demonstrated that fact for me. "But they'd just catch me again, and next time the punishment would be worse. Know what it is? You have to eat *pesto!*" He made a horrible face.

I continued across the square to what in New York would have been a multiple dwellingplace of modest size. With its half-dozen stories, it was the largest building hereabout. I could see some sort of placard on its front doors. If government was to be found on the square, this seemed most likely to be where.

When I reached the sign, which was crudely made of cardboard and inscribed in felt-penned capitals, I read:

W.C.—3RD FLOOR FRONT
CHAMBER OF LEGISLATORS—3RD FL. FRONT
MINISTRIES—ATTIC
COURT OF JUSTICE—CELLAR

Nearby, on the wall of the building, was a proper brass sign which discreetly proclaimed the presence, in the same edifice, of Dr. C. Moritz, Podiatrist; Mellenkamp & Co., Novelties; The Brockden School of Ventriloquism; and the House of Costumes.

Of the governmental tenants, the Court was most quickly reached from the ground floor. The one-car elevator at the rear of the little lobby seemed indifferent to my button-pushing, and therefore I went beyond it to a staircase and descended to a dank basement corridor, which was dimly lighted by a naked bulb of small wattage that hung from the ceiling on a badly frayed wire. I groped my way along the hallway, trudging here and there through pools of standing water and more than once hearing scurryings that could have come only from rodents of a fairly substantial size.

I had begun to assume I was in the wrong cellar for the Court, or else the handwritten sign outside had been the work of a practical joker with unfathomable motives, and was about to turn back when a door opened in the crepuscularity just beyond me, and an ancient man, with a parchment skull around which were a few unruly wisps of white hair, shuffled forth. His judicial robes were tattered.

I was amazed that he could see me, given his rheumy eyes and the feeble available light. "*Now* you come," he said peevishly. "Now, when I've got to go piss. Well, you'll just have to wait while I go to the toilet, which means climbing the stairs, for the lift is once again out of order, and then at my age you have to stand there till the prostate gland decides what to do, holding that shriveled wick that's no earthly good for any other function."

"I was simply going to observe the court at work," I said. "Please don't feel any need to hurry on my account. I'll just go in and sit down. Is anyone else there?"

"Certainly not," said he. "We dispense swift justice here and don't make people wait around."

"Then I'll come upstairs with you and look in on the other branches of government while you're in the toilet."

He made a gesture of indifference. Going up the stairs at his side required more patience than I had anticipated, so slow and tottering was his climb, but when I offered him a hand or arm, his rejection, with a horny elbow, smote my ribs that were still sore from the calipers of Olga's steel thighs.

To make some use of this time I asked him about the court: was it civil or criminal?

He grunted disagreeably. "What a dumb question. Criminals have no place in a court! They are dealt with by the police."

"But is it not possible that the police might sometime punish the wrong man?"

"It's also possible that a person might be struck by lightning or have some other kind of ill fortune, contract a mortal illness, and so on, but that sort of thing is not an occasion for a resort to a court of justice."

"Then what does your court deal with? Civil lawsuits?"

By now we had climbed perhaps four steps, each of which the

old jurist gained in a most precarious way, teetering interminably on the metal binding at the edge of the tread and arresting a backwards fall with a desperate grasp of the rail, applied only at the last moment it could have been effective. After witnessing this procedure repeatedly I at last took my heart from my mouth: he was actually in no danger of falling.

"I don't know what that term means," said he. "What I adjudicate are private differences between individuals. For example, a man acquires a new possession, say a pocketknife, and proudly shows it to a friend. The friend disparages it, so the owner of the knife hauls him into court on a charge of envy. The defendant, on the other hand, tries to prove that his criticism of the knife had to do only with objective standards of quality: the workmanship is shoddy by comparison with other knives sold for the same amount of money."

"Suppose you decided in favor of the plaintiff in this example?"

"If the decision went against the defendant, he would be obliged, for a certain length of time, to wear a placard on his back announcing to the world that he was an envious person."

"The same kind of thing, then, that the person arrested for rudeness must undergo."

"Not at all. Rudeness is a crime against the state," said the old judge. "Envy is a personal matter. An envious man is not put into the pillory."

I couldn't see the distinction. Therefore I asked him another question. "Do you have insurance companies in Saint Sebastian?"

"No," said he. "It is against the law to wager on someone else's misfortune."

"Then what happens to the man on whose sidewalk a pedestrian slips and breaks his collarbone and subsequently sues the property owner: a routine occurrence in the States—?" Something like that happened to a retired postman who lived next door to my uncle's sister-in-law's second cousin's friend: the uninsured ex-mailman was the defendant; the victim claimed he had dislocated his spine; I never learned of the outcome.

"Yes," said the old man, toiling up the third-to-last step to the ground floor. "The victim would surely be sued by the property owner."

"Can I have heard you correctly? The *victim* would be sued? Wouldn't he be doing the suing?"

His glare suggested such annoyance that I was concerned lest he become distracted and lose his tenuous grasp of the railing and plunge backwards down the stairs. "Are you trying to bait me?"

"Forgive me, sir. I'm honestly trying to understand the workings of your law, so different from ours. In America, and I think many other places, the injured party is the plaintiff."

"And so with us," the old man told me, his anger subsiding, or rather turning into what would seem contempt. "In the episode you have projected, the property owner would have been humiliated by someone's having been injured on his sidewalk. It would only be right that he sued the fellow who was responsible, *viz.*, he whose back was injured."

"But what of the victim? First he hurt his spine and is perhaps permanently disabled, and then he is sued. Is that justice?"

The judge's brow descended. "Yes," said he. "The person you speak of sounds as if he might definitely be the kind of unfortunate whose specialty is making the people around him totally miserable. One more such outrage might well prove him to be the kind of troublemaker we would want to eliminate from our society."

I repeated, "Eliminate?" The problem with ingenious systems of justice is that they inevitably have their ugly aspect.

"It's often the only answer," said he. We had at last reached the lobby, where he stood sourly contemplating the door of the out-of-service elevator. "And Gezieferland, believe it or not, dotes on such people: they're always after us to send them more losers. Sometimes they even threaten to go to war. The idea there is that we'd beat them savagely and thus their entire population would again suffer the kind of loss they live for."

As I remembered from Olga's remarks, Gezieferland was another little country, north of Saint Sebastian. "Are you saying that you exile these so-called losers to your northern neighbor?"

He nodded, and proceeded to refer to the southern neighbor mentioned by Olga. "Swatina takes off our hands anyone who makes a public menace of himself: say, walks along the street speaking violently to an invisible companion or exposes a part of himself that might disgust others, such as a back covered with pimples or an enormous belly. There are scoundrels, male and female, who will commit this crime at the beach and play portable phonographs and eat gluttonously while dripping with sweat. Lying to the south of us, Swatina has a warmer climate than we and consequently a longer beach season. Indeed, the visitor to that wretched country sees nothing but striped umbrellas and hideous naked bodies."

My physical impatience was making me uncomfortable. I could not endure creeping up two more floors in his company. Therefore, with thanks to him for helping me to a new understanding of Saint Sebastian, I hastened to a narrow flight of upward-leading stairs and climbed to what Americans would have called the second floor, but which, in the European style, was the first: of this I was reminded by the painted *1* on the wall of the landing. This meant that the old judge would have an even longer climb to the toilet than I had first supposed.

It seemed nonsensical that the governmental agencies would be put on the upper floors when a costume business, a school of ventriloquism, and the novelties of Mellenkamp occupied the more accessible offices. I thought that on the route upstairs I might just stop off at one or more of these establishments and talk with the people who worked there, but on each landing there was a locked door between the stairway and the business floor, as well as a sign forbidding entry and warning the would-be trespasser that attack dogs patrolled the premises at all hours.

At the third (actually the fourth) floor, the door to the landing stood open. To shut it would have been preposterous: it consisted of an empty frame from which the panels had been removed. I went along the corridor, passing the toilets (which had no doors whatever and therefore no designation as to the sex of their users). I arrived at a door marked CHAMBER OF LEGISLATORS. I opened it and stepped inside.

What I saw was a largish room filled with canvas cots of the folding, Army type, each of which contained the recumbent form of a markedly shabby man. The odor of the place was very unpleasant. As I stood there, surveying the place, I felt a hand plucking at my trousers in the area of the knee. It was the man on the nearest bunk.

"Hey, buddy," said he, continuing to yank at me, "gimme some dope." He seemed not much older than I, but he was in miserable physical condition, and he obviously had not washed his face in time out of mind: the dirt was ingrained.

"I don't have any," I said, and pulled away from his grasp.

"How about a drink?" When I shook my head, he asked, "Then have you got a cigarette at least?"

"Sorry, I don't smoke."

"Then what *have* you got for your legislator?" he asked. "It better be good, if you want me to scratch *your* back."

"I'm a visitor, a foreigner. Are you really a legislator?"

"If you're not one of my constituents, go fuck yourself," said he, letting his head fall back on the unspeakably filthy pillow.

As it happened I was not offended, but I *was* curious. "You have no interest in maintaining friendly relations with other countries?"

He replied without bothering to raise his head. "I might or might not have, according to my needs at the moment, but being nice to you would have nothing to do with the matter in any event."

"You mean because I come from a country that has a long record of rewarding those who insult it?"

"I don't know or care which country you belong to," said the recumbent legislator. "I'm speaking universally. And that has exhausted me." He closed his eyes and almost immediately began to snore, denying me the opportunity to ask him a final question.

Therefore I put it to the man in the next bunk, a person quite as filthy as the first and as disagreeable, who sneered at me and said, "Keep going. I heard what you said to Filtschmidt."

"I merely wanted to ask why you have no fear of being arrested for rudeness."

"Because we're legislators, you cretin. Why should we create a law to which we ourselves are subject?"

By now these people had succeeded in irking me. "According to my information," I said with a sneer of my own, "you have no power whatever."

He covered his eyes and wept, the tears running abundantly from beneath his hands to drip on the dirty, caseless pillow, as if he were squeezing water from a concealed sponge. When at last he spoke, he did so through sobs.

"I have never been addressed so cruelly." He wept some more. "Oh, how could you?"

I had enough. "Stop that sniveling, you ninny. You reserve the right to be nasty to others, but you can't take your own medicine."

"But that's the only way of doing it!" he howled. "You're punishing me for being human, and it isn't fair!"

"If you were brighter," said I, "you would understand that my punishing you is only human, as well, and it's really not fair of you to call me unfair."

At least he stopped crying. Now he simply looked baffled. I decided that further traffic with the legislators would not be fruitful, and I left the smelly dormitory, found the stairway again, and climbed until I reached the attic. Judging from the many steps I encountered, the attic was three or four stories above the legislators' chamber, but I found no indication en route that I was passing other floors and saw no means of access to them if indeed they were in place.

At the top of the stairway was a door of which the top panel was frosted glass. Scotch-taped to my side was a typewritten notice, which read:

> BEYOND THIS DOOR ARE THE ROYAL MINISTRIES. ALL PERSONS ARE HEREBY WARNED THAT ANY VISITOR MAY BE ASSAULTED AT ANY TIME AT THE WHIM OF THE MINISTERS, WHO ARE NOTHING IF NOT WILLFUL.

This news was not reassuring, but I had expended too much energy to turn back now. I opened the door and walked down a brightly lighted corridor of which the walls were painted a cheery apple-green. The hallway was carpeted in a slightly darker version of the same color. These premises were the most attractive I had yet found in the building, and but for the sign outside I would have assumed I had succeeded in penetrating not a governmental office but rather one of the business floors I had elsewhere been denied admittance to.

The first door on my right, made of solid wood and painted in a jolly French blue, was labeled: MINISTRY OF IRONY. I decided to go along the hall to its termination and see what the other ministries were called, before choosing which to enter first. The next, on the left, with a door of bright orange, was the Ministry of Disaffection. Then came, on the right, the Ministry of Clams. On the left again, the Ministry of Allergies. The doors to the foregoing were painted, respectively, blue-green and brick red. Finally, at the end of the hall, neither right nor left, but facing the visitor, was a zebra-striped black-and-white door labeled: MINISTRY OF HOAXES.

I confess I could not resist applying first at the last-named. I was rewarded by the sight of a very comely redhaired young woman, who sat at a receptionist's desk in an anteroom furnished with deep chairs and an outsized sofa. These pieces were upholstered in salt-'n'-pepper nubby tweeds. Here and there on the walls were hung *trompe-l'oeil* still lifes which at any distance at all you could have sworn were real: the dead pheasant, next to the game bag and fowling piece, seemed really to be decaying.

"How do you do," I said to the receptionist. "I'm a visitor to your country. I wonder whether you'd be willing to tell me something about this ministry? Am I correct in assuming that its work is rather like that of what in America we call the police bunco squad? Do you deal with the kind of misrepresentation by which honest citizens are bilked?"

She smiled at me. "We don't *police* hoaxes, we practice them. For example, we spend the money allocated to us for one purpose on something else entirely. We pretend to be a vast bureau with hundreds of employees, but in reality there's just me and Albert."

"Albert's the minister?"

"No, he's the bouncer." And then, no doubt owing to my puzzled expression, she explained. "Some people—though by no means all—are resentful when they discover they've been tricked. If they bring their complaints here, Albert is the man who deals with them."

"I see." More brutality. "Well, thank you for—" I realized that I was beginning to smell a nauseating odor. . . . Of course, that pheasant in the fool-the-eye painting *was* real and decaying!

What an unpleasant place the Ministry of Hoaxes had proved to be. However, male pride with respect to the redheaded receptionist would not let me leave on a sinking note. I took a conspicuously deep breath and winked at the picture.

"By George, that's so clever you'd swear it was phony."

"It is," said the young woman. "Step closer."

I obeyed her and found, after all, only a painted bird. "It's so believable," I confessed, "that I was sure I could smell it."

"You could," she said in what I was finding an insufferable smugness. "The odor is piped in through a vent."

"What's the purpose of such a thing?"

She extended a glistening underlip. "Look, duping people is our job. If you have a complaint, talk to Albert." Before I could discourage her, she pressed a bell push mounted at the edge of her desk, and immediately a door opened behind her and a man came out of the inner office.

But to my relief I saw he was a small, frail-looking person, a good ten to fifteen years older than I. He wore a genial smile. I recognized that the hoax here was that one would be threatened with "the bouncer," and then harmless Albert would appear and discuss your problem in a reasonable, even sympathetic way, utterly unlike any governmental employee I had ever met back home, beginning with the mailman, who, since my failure to reward him lavishly enough one Xmas, had habitually left my packages in the entryway corner where winos urinated.

"How do you do, sir?" Albert greeted me. "Do you have a complaint?"

"Perhaps I do, at that," I replied. "Doesn't government, any government, practice enough hoaxing in the ordinary course of its activity as to make pointless a special ministry for the purpose?"

His smile became even warmer. "But don't you see how useful it is to have one government agency which candidly states, boasts, that its function is solely to gull the citizen. We practice pure hoaxing for hoaxing's sake, with no ulterior motive. We don't pretend to deal with national highways, for example, or the exchequer, agriculture, or whatnot, and then instead play cards, drink beer, and read thrillers the day long, as they do in Gezieferland. No, we do our job straightforwardly and we're proud of it. You have any contact with us, and you'll be bamboozled or know the reason why. Speak to any Sebastianer and you will find that we are that ministry most trusted by the public."

As with so many of the phenomena I had encountered in this country, what had seemed utterly preposterous at the outset had a milligram or two of reason in it when more closely examined, but rarely if ever enough to bring it even into the neighborhood of the desirable.

"Very well," I said, "you have explained it."

His smile grew cooler. "But you're not yet convinced, are you?"

"Oh, I wouldn't say that—" At this point Albert gave me a powerful one-two punch to the midsection. As I bent to favor the pain my legs gave way, and I crumpled to the carpet. I did not genuinely pass out, but, appropriately enough for this office, I simulated unconsciousness so that he would not give me a taste of his heavy shoes, which in close-up looked as though they might be capped with metal.

After he returned to the inner room, I laboriously regained my footing and limped to the exit door.

"Thank you for calling at the Ministry," the redhead said behind me. "We're always glad to help."

I decided to pass up both the ministry that dealt with irony and that whose business was disaffection, for I believed, projecting from my experience at Hoaxes, that I could imagine more or less what they were up to. But I must say I was curious about the ministries of, respectively, Clams and Allergies, if for no other reason than their incongruity with each other and, indeed, everything else.

The office was like that which I had only just left, but this time the receptionist was a young man with a handlebar mustache.

"Good afternoon," said he. "May I help you?"

After identifying myself, I asked him what was the precise function of his ministry. "Clam fishing is obviously one of the important pursuits in your country. I wasn't even aware that you had access to any ocean and was amazed at the variety of offerings at the open-air seafood market."

"We have no coastline," said he. "Our only water is the river, which of course provides no clams. Trout, eels, gudgeon, and some other freshwater fish are caught in the river by individuals for their own private use and are not sold to the public. That display in the market is artificial: the seafood is made of plastic."

After a moment I nodded. "Uh-huh, that would explain the absence of any odor. . . . OK, then: you have no clams in Saint Sebastian."

"That's correct," said he. "Which is why we have the ministry."

"I confess I haven't the beginning of an understanding."

"Aha," he said, flicking the left tip of his mustache, as if dislodging a fly. "Nothing could be simpler or more effective as an instrument of government than a ministry of clams. It has but one function: it is the bureau of last resort, to which all insoluble problems are sent, to which all unanswerable complaints are forwarded. If nothing can be done about something, for example a plague of locusts at a time when there is an inexplicable absence of the kinds of birds that eat large insects and atmospheric conditions forbid the use of insecticides. If the crops are destroyed the farmers can curse fate, but for their emotional well-being they really need some human agency to blame. The Ministry of Clams serves such a purpose. Accepting denunciations is our job. Look here."

He rose from the desk and opened the door to the inner office. I came to the threshold and looked in. The sizable room I saw was filled from wall to wall with metal filing cabinets, with just enough space between their ranks for the drawers to be opened.

"Those cabinets," said the mustachioed receptionist, "contain the complaints received for the past thirty days. On the first of next month they will be emptied for the reception of a new consignment."

"Your efficiency is breathtaking," I said. "How do you manage to deal with such a volume of work in only a month?"

"By doing nothing whatever about it but filing the papers!" he cried. "Is that not beautiful?"

"And the complainants are satisfied?"

He frowned. "No, one cannot make such a statement, for human beings, whatever their situation, are *never* satisfied. Trying to make them so is a waste of effort, perhaps even a mockery of the human condition. Have you ever known any social problem that was truly solved?"

"Let me think. Of course, the child labor that was the disgrace of the early Industrial Revolution. Humane laws did away with it."

"And the result was a child population consisting of illiterate dope addicts supported by government handouts."

"Oh, come on. You exaggerate."

He nodded soberly. "You're right. Those who became criminals were very prosperous."

"Living in New York has made me a monster of cynicism," I said, "but surely you go too far."

"I'm speaking not of your country," said the young man, "but rather of mine, as it was back in the Dark Ages, before the Enlightenment, which brought among other things the Ministry of Clams."

"Am I right in suspecting that your so-called Enlightenment was not all that far in the past?"

"Indeed you are," said he. "For some reason, it is the fashion to call that period the Sixties, though in fact virtually all the important reforms happened rather in the Seventies."

"And what role does the prince play in all of this?"

"None whatever," said the young man. "I doubt that he even knows of the existence of our ministry."

"Remarkable!" I exclaimed. "Do you receive many complaints with reference to him?"

"Never. It's impossible to complain of the prince. He's beyond it all, like the flag."

I told him I had never yet seen the flag of Saint Sebastian.

"No, and you probably never will. I have never seen it though I'm native born and work for the government. I believe it's kept in some top-secret place along with the Constitution. I've never heard who has access to them. Maybe they don't even exist!"

"Like the poetry of which your leading critic writes," I suggested.

"Isn't that fun?" he asked, smiling with a set of horsey front teeth.

"Just two more questions, if you will. Why do you use the word 'clams'?"

"To suggest the ministry's true function in its name would strike a negative note. We could have called it something else, I suppose: the 'Ministry of Aubergines,' for example, but that sounds too frivolous. The 'Ministry of Rust,' on the other hand, has an ugly sound. No, we think 'Clams' strikes the right note. There's the pleasant connotation 'happy as a clam.' And any suggestion that encourages the populace to be discreet and not circulate gossip is welcome: I refer of course to 'clamming up.' Fortunately, most Sebastianers are innocent of your World War Two GI term for the female organ, unless like me they have been instructed by Mr. McCoy: the 'bearded clam.' "

Embarrassed, I said hastily, "Yes, he's a scholar in the vocabulary of vintage obscenity. In fact, at the moment he's putting together a comprehensive lexicon of indecent terms for the press of one of our leading universities. . . . My other question pertains to your artificial fish market. Why do you have such a thing?"

"Because it is colorful," said he. "Because fish markets are traditional, and why should we be denied one simply because we are far from any coast and wish to be self-sufficient and eat only those foods we find or grow in our own land? But mostly so that we might have fishwives."

"Fishwives?"

"Who can scream more loudly or demonstrate a more authoritative use of invective? Having such a spectacle available at all times is a healthy thing for a society."

I thanked the young man for his eloquent presentation. "Could you give me some idea of the function of the Ministry of Allergies? I'm not sure I have enough time for a visit there."

He grimaced. "I'd stay away if I were you. It's an unpleasant place. I wouldn't work there on a bet, though I realize it's necessary, for even in salubrious Saint Sebastian some people fall ill, some even die, though of course everything concerning death is kept under the hat."

"Could you explain?"

"If a certain person doesn't show up for several days, without having left some message as to his whereabouts, the assumption is he's dead."

"His near and dear, however, surely know?"

"Certainly not," said the young man with the mustache, "unless they, or someone else for that matter, has been present at his death, which after all could happen from a bolt of lightning or by falling off a mountain. But you can be sure that, if so, they would keep mum about it, for nothing is more severely punished than to speak of such a matter."

"But most deaths result from illness, I'm sure, and not accidents."

"*Allergies,*" said he, "which are, all of them, at bottom but one: an allergy to living."

"All matters pertaining to illness are the business of the Ministry of Allergies?"

"Yes."

"And death as well?"

He shook his head. "No. Death has its own department: the Ministry of Irony."

As usual I was taken by surprise. In this case I had too easily assumed that at Irony the bureaucrats sat around exchanging cynical wisecracks.

My final question was as to the function of the Ministry of Disaffection.

The young man piously rolled his eyes at the ceiling. "You must not pass it up."

"Really? Well, then, I'll stop by." I thanked him and left.

I went along the hallway to the orange door. Just as I was about to touch the knob, it receded, and a thin, sour-looking woman of about fifty years of age appeared in the narrow opening between the door and frame and said, with a kind of melancholy peevishness, "We don't want any."

"I'm not a salesman, madame. I'm a visitor from abroad."

"But we don't *want* a visitor," said she. "What good would you do us?"

This was a challenge. "I neglected to mention that I'm an American. My country is thinking of giving money to yours."

"Money wouldn't do us any good," she said, shaking her head of iron-gray hair tightly pinned. "We'd just spend it."

"I believe that's the idea with money."

"If we spent it, we wouldn't have it long, so what would be the point of receiving it in the first place? If it was just one gift, however large, it would soon be gone, and the lack of money, after having had a taste of it, would be degenerating. On the other hand, if you continued to provide money, we'd become your helpless parasites in no time at all."

"OK, then," I said with all the good nature I could summon up. "Forget money. I just want to be your friend."

She frowned for a while, as if in thought, and then said, while shutting the door, "I don't see any profit in that."

8

On my way downstairs I encountered the ancient judge, who stood catching his breath on the landing at the entrance to the third floor. Apparently he had not yet reached the toilet, for he was facing in, not out. He stared disapprovingly at me, giving no indication that we had met before, and therefore I did not seek to converse with him now.

As I went along the street I came to a building which was identified, on a polished brass plate alongside its front door, as The Linden Street School. The cable clerk had mentioned this institution. Curiosity took me inside its entrance hall, which proved to be a lobby decorated with colorful posters of coming cinematic attractions.

"Come along, come along!" said an impatient voice. "The feature is just starting." This command was directed to me by a woman dressed as a nun, who stood at a curtain-draped doorway. When I approached she held the curtain aside and switched on the small flashlight she carried and preceded me down the aisle. I had never before received this sort of service at a movie house, but could recall seeing the like in vintage films, in which a hero, seeking to hide out till some ill wind blew past, took similar refuge in a cinema, as in real life did our latest successful presidential assassin.

I wanted to continue on to my habitual place, rather nearer the screen than would be the taste of most, owing to a mild myopia, but the stern sister forced me to take an aisle seat no more than halfway along, reminding me that I had "a job to do." I had no sense of what she meant until I sat down. Immediately I was asked for permission to go to the toilet. My eyes not having as yet adjusted to the darkness, I could not identify either the sex or the age of this personage in the seat next mine, but the voice was that of a child.

"Why do you ask me?"

"Because you're the monitor!" said the person whose small body was climbing over my legs before I could begin to stand up.

I became aware that all this while there had been images on and sound emanating from the screen. I now took conscious note of these and saw that the black-and-white Coming Attractions were just ending in a riot of giant display type, followed by exclamation marks and printed on the diagonal. Whatever was on its way to this theater next would be SHOCKING!!!

But then the titles began for the feature, and I was incredulous when I saw, after the name and logo of the studio had come and gone (for the record, "Puma Productions" and a cougar who bared his fangs at the camera), "Ben Spinoza . . . in . . . GATS 'N' GALS," the actor and title I had created from thin air so as to defend myself when speaking with the cable clerk!

By now my vision was clearing, and therefore I could discern, when the nun returned her, fingers pincered on her ear, that my toilet-bound neighbor was about eight years old, had a short butcher-boy haircut, and was dressed in the kind of smock worn by French schoolchildren.

While the girl climbed back to her seat, the nun upbraided me for letting the child out of the aisle.

"For a person of your age to be taken in by such an old ruse is ridiculous," said the sister. "Nobody leaves their seat *till the end of the picture!*"

After she left, the little girl said, "Sorry. I didn't mean to get you in trouble. But I really hate gangster pictures."

I was touched by this manifestation of decency in a human being of such a tender age—before I reflected, New Yorkly, that if you don't find it in a child, you won't see it anywhere.

"What kind of movies do you like?"

"Where the ladies are rich and have servants waiting on them and wear pretty clothes, and where the men have their hair combed and wear those coats with the long backs and fancy shirts and they help the ladies into carriages and they go to places with shining candles and dance in two lines, one for the ladies and one for the men."

How I used to hate it when at her age I would be trapped at a costume picture with such tedious sissy-scenes, which one must endure so as to reach the swordfights.

"It takes all kinds," I told her.

Gats 'n' Gals proved to be somewhat better than I anticipated. Its morality was oversimplistic, but it was a relief, after all these years, to see criminals presented as deplorable creatures while the men of law enforcement were courageous, honorable, and even courteous (while routinely wearing their wide-brimmed fedoras indoors, they doffed them when a woman entered the room). The dialogue would provide more grist for the cable clerk's linguistic mill: cigarettes were "coffin nails"; women, "twists"; cars, "chariots"; and clothes, faces, and dollars were, respectively, "duds," "mugs," and "simoleons." Spinoza was a middle-sized chap, on the slender side, but with a thrusting jaw. At one point he fist-fought two thugs who (in addition to being giants) pressed into service as weapons a series of found objects, chairs, lengths of pipe, and an axe, but with the use of only his two hands Ben eventually "closed out their accounts," to quote a line of his partner, another G-man, who is subsequently shot in the back by a dastardly, toadlike ruffian, but who has recovered sufficiently by the end of the film to receive a hospital bedside visit from his winsome sister, who has fallen hard for Spinoza, but in the convention of the time had behaved snippily towards him until he appears now, with a box of candy for the invalid and a boyish grin for her. "I'll bet I know who'd make a swell best man!" says she, simpering at her brother, whose eyebrows rise in a benevolent amazement that is surely also ingenuous.

No sooner had "The End" appeared on the screen than I was treated as an inanimate obstacle not only by the little girl from the seat next me, but by all the children in the row: they climbed, vaulted, swarmed, over me and pushed into the general congestion of the aisle, which was clogged with other children and, farther along, the adults who had occupied the seats more distant from the screen.

I detained, against his will, the last child to leave my row, and was informed by him, in answer to my question, that this was a toilet break and not the end of what he thought of as the schoolday.

"There are more movies?"

He portrayed disgust with his mouth and nose. "Where've *you* been all your life? We don't get out till five. We've still got to watch a chapter of a Tim McCoy serial, an Edgar Kennedy comedy, and some dumb girls' picture with singing and dancing!"

He wriggled away and plunged into the aisle-traffic before I could ask him more. I waited until the throng had passed and then left my seat. Before I could reach the street, however, I was stopped by the stern-faced nun who had chided me earlier.

"Because of the allergies that are going round, we'll be shorthanded for monitors again at the evening session, and you'll have to stay."

"Excuse me?"

"I think I'm speaking clearly enough," said she, lengthening the lines that ran from the base of her nose to the mouth. She was one of those persons who have forever the power to make one feel feckless. "You have a job to do."

"As it happens, Sister, I am an American visitor who just wandered into the school by chance."

This information made her no more genial. "Then tell me if you can," said she, "why your films are of such poor quality. Some are scratched badly, and many break during a screening, and Father has to stop the machine and splice the film. At such times the children can become quite unruly. Even our adult-education groups get restless."

"You must understand, I am not connected with the American film industry and have little technical knowledge, but I wonder whether your troubles might not be due to the age of the pictures. From what I understand, the movies you show are almost half a century old. *Gats 'n' Gals*, for example, obviously dates from before World War Two."

She squinted suspiciously at me. "Can that be true?"

"Oh yes. I can assure you that if indeed he is still alive, Ben Spinoza is quite an old man. Those boxlike cars are seen only at the exhibitions given by collectors, and the clothes worn by both criminals and law-enforcers would nowadays not be seen publicly on anyone except perhaps the kind of alternative-sex people who go to parties given by celebrity designers."

The nun looked even more grim. "I wonder whether Father knows this." She beckoned to me. "Come along."

I supposed I was not really obliged to obey her, but, as I say, her air of authority was that authentic kind that requires more of an effort to dismiss than to honor. I followed her black habit and white cowl through a little door and up a flight of stairs and into a projection room in which were twin movie machines, other pieces of equipment, and a balding man wearing a round collar. The last-named sat at a table in front of a film-editing device: two reels separated by a glass screen. I vaguely remembered seeing a smaller version of such a gadget in the "den" of an uncle who was familially notorious as a home-movie bore, who with his intrusive camera would delay holiday meals until the food grew cold and never fail to catch for eternity any minor embarrassment within the 360-degree purview of his lens, while missing altogether the local events of great moment (tornadoes, presidential motorcades, circus processions with prancing bears).

The nun spoke. "I'm sorry to bother you, Father, but this American has quite a story to tell."

The priest continued to stare silently into the glass window of the machine before him, while slowly turning the right-hand reel by means of the little crank attached to it.

I didn't like the implication that what I had to say might be questionable, and bridled when the sister made it even stronger. "You won't believe this, but I really do think you might want to hear it." She gave me a bleak look. "Go ahead."

"I don't have earth-shattering news to relate, I'm afraid, but the American films you show are of an earlier era and do not reflect the current life of my country."

Without looking up from his gadget the priest said, "I'm well aware of that."

I looked at the nun. She said, "*I* wasn't." She made a quiet exit.

"An usherette doesn't have to be," murmured the man of the cloth, shaking his head at something he saw in the little screen. "I don't know how many more splices this will take." At last he looked up at me. "That's the only trouble, the physical condition of many of these pictures. We could use some new copies. You don't suppose that when you go back home you might look for somebody who could make copies of these fine films? We don't have adequate equipment for that job over here. No doubt they might elsewhere in Europe, but we Sebastianers don't like to admit our weaknesses to anyone nearby."

"I suppose I could do that," I said. "But could you tell me where you get these films nowadays?"

"Aha." He had keen eyes under metal-rimmed spectacles and was losing his hair at those two places on the crown just above the temples. "Your USO and Army people left them behind when they went home after World War Two. It seems that Mr. McCoy had access to them. Were it not for these pictures I don't know what our Enlightenment could have come to."

"I confess I find it curious that the clergy of all people would condone the exchanging of schools and churches for cinemas."

The priest laughed merrily. " 'Condoned' is too mild a word, my dear fellow! We were positively ecstatic to do so. For the first time in a century we have full houses!"

"And the movies are also a substitute for school?"

He frowned. "The choice of words is not appropriate. The movies are not substitutes! If anything, church and school were the substitutes. They were poor imitations of life. Now we can see the real thing."

"Old American films are the real thing?"

"Yes, of course," the priest said forcefully. "The virtuous are shown to succeed, the evildoers invariably come to grief, and the general philosophy that informs every picture is that there is a common good, which is recognized by everyone—including the wicked, who of course are opposed to it, but they *know what it is.* Believe it or not, before the Enlightenment, Sebastiani society had no such standards or beliefs. The church had utterly different aims from the schools, and the code one learned in each was utterly confounded by one's experience of life. And the government received no respect from anyone, which of course is still true, but now the government is *intentionally* performed as a farce, and is quite effective."

"Namely, it does nothing."

His smile became ever more radiant. "Exactly! And are you aware of what an achievement that is? Unprecedented throughout history! Not even the Austro-Hungarians were able quite to pull that off."

"And everything is run on credit."

"One of the most brilliant schemes man has ever devised!" said he. "And not all that different from the old way of exchanging pieces of paper, if you think of it. A bank note has no intrinsic value, nor has a check. And it has been a long time, has it not, since the coins circulated in any country have had much value as metal? All the foregoing means of payment are essentially no more than credit, eh?"

Until now, being in my peculiar situation, I had not thought of an obvious question, *viz.*, "Who decides who gets most credit?"

The priest had gone back to his movie-viewer. He now looked up with a quizzical expression. "Credit is unlimited for everybody."

"Then everybody is rich?"

"Far from it," said he. "We have fewer rich people than we formerly had, and of course many fewer of the poor. But some of those who *are* rich are richer than they were previously, and there are still *some* poor people."

"And could you explain that, Father?" It might seem ridiculous that I so addressed a projectionist, but the fact was that, like the nun, the priest seemed to retain all the authority he would ever have had.

"Personal taste," he said. "There really is an enormous variation amongst human beings. One exercises his vanity in quite another way than that of his neighbor: one by accumulation, the next by deprivation. But of course most Sebastianers, so as to allay envy, are somewhere in the middle."

"Then vanity and envy were not eradicated by the Enlightenment?"

The priest grimaced at me. "Are you really so naïve, or should I take that question as derisive?"

I admitted, "I really can't decide."

His brow cleared. He accepted that answer in good humor, perhaps because he understood that it was no more or less than the truth (unless I am being too sentimental in my assessment of him, as those reared as liberal Protestants tend to be with respect to a celibate clergy).

"I'll withdraw the question and put another," I told him. "What do you think of the Blonds?"

"They are all God's children."

"I meant their situation in society."

He shrugged. "I don't know what to say beyond 'There it is.' "

"Are they not condemned by the mere fact of their birth? Is a person responsible for the color of the hair with which he was born?"

The priest stared at me. "No, of course not, but he certainly is for that which he retains as an adult."

"What does that mean?"

"Most of us are *born* with fair hair," he said resentfully. "Our parents dye it throughout childhood and then when we become adults we either continue the practice ourselves, if we have any self-respect, or go rotten and allow it to return to what it was, which gives a moral weakling a further excuse to make nothing of himself. Nobody expects anything of the fairhaired, you see. It's a self-fulfilling kind of thing."

If this was true, then the argument of Olga and the other liberationists was necessarily compromised, but now the negative side of my basic sense of priests came into play: were they not professional defenders of whichever status was quo, provided it included them?

"The Blonds, then, deserve what they get?"

"I'd put it another way," said he. "They get what they give every evidence of wanting."

"Thank you, Father. I've profited by our little talk. By the way, in your current job do you still take confessions?"

"Of course. People nowadays call them in on the telephone, thereby being able better to conceal their identities and at the same time allowing us to transmit their remarks on the radio."

"You don't mean the confessions are broadcast?"

"Yes, indeed, and the program is perennially the most popular. The excitement is in what each show will bring. No one knows. They're not rigged or edited in any way, but go on as they come over the phone. You might get twenty or more innocuous ones or nothing more than impure thoughts before a really filthy story comes along. You never can tell."

"By 'filthy' you mean . . . ?"

"Do you think I would repeat such smut aloud?" he asked indignantly.

"I haven't heard television mentioned since I got here," I said.

"The radio engineers are working on it," said the priest. "But it'll be a while before it gets to be more than a novelty."

I thanked him again and left. On the main floor I encountered the nun again. She was directing the traffic of children and adults on their return to the auditorium, but left off for a moment to ask me, though I was foreigner, to serve again as monitor for the next picture, which starred someone named John Boles, but I expressed my regrets and departed from the building.

No sooner had I stepped into the street than two men moved against me, one from either side, and in a pincer-play conducted me to the curb, against which a long black automobile that might have been a vintage Mercedes suddenly swooped in from nowhere. The rear door was flung open and I was pushed inside, one man climbing in after, and the other going around to enter from the opposite door. My captors were of a similar height and weight and wore identical black suits.

This sequence had occurred too swiftly for me as yet to have reacted, pondering as I had been, at the moment of capture, on the educational system of Saint Sebastian, but I was ready by the time the car started to roll.

"How dare you?" I demanded first of one man, and then turned and repeated it to the other. Their being dressed identically was taxing: I found I had to guard against the tendency to repeat to either whatever I had said to the other, though they were separated only by the width of my person. Only by the rigid application of self-discipline was I able to establish a style in which the first part of any utterance was addressed to the man on my left and the second to him on the right. As for example, what I said next.

"Who are you?" Turn. "And where are you taking me?"

The questions were answered with twin silences. The car was

being driven by a man with thickset shoulders and a neck that was as wide as that part of his head I could see before it vanished into his hat. The car was moving too swiftly for me to attempt an escape from it while it was in motion; therefore I persisted in my attempts at conversation, this time taking a more leisurely tack.

"Do you know"—turn—"this is the only car I've seen on the streets"—turn—"other than that of Mr. McCoy, the expatriate American journalist"—turn—"whom you may"—turn—"know, given"—turn—"the small size of this country."

Neither of them acknowledged any of this, and soon the car entered a courtyard and pulled up before a gloomy-looking stone building of fortresslike construction: those few windows it had were narrow and barred. The two men hustled me into its grim dark interior, along several tunneled corridors ever grimmer and darker, and finally into a room that was grimmest, and darkest, of all, illuminated at the moment only by whatever light could penetrate the slit-window high on the wall, though a lamp with a mesh-covered reflector hung from the ceiling directly over the single piece of furniture in the room, a stark straightbacked chair.

I was pushed violently towards the chair and told to sit upon it. The overhead light was switched on. The bulb was more powerful than I expected; I sat in a cone of intense light, and the heat of it was comforting, for the men soon left the room. How long I sat there I could not say, but finally the door opened and in came a person I could hardly see: he remained in the shadows beyond the circle of light.

Suddenly he said in a harsh tone, "You've been frequenting a Blond."

"I'm a tourist."

"You're an American agent."

"May I ask who *you* are?"

"The State Security Service of Saint Sebastian."

I suspected my best move would be to tell the literal truth, up to a point. "By chance I encountered the stewardess of the airplane that brought me here. 'Frequenting' is scarcely the word for my distant and brief acquaintance with her."

"You did not fuck her? Blond females are nymphomaniacs."

He came closer, but I still could not see him except in outline. "Oh, you fucked her," said he, "or vice versa."

I took the courage to say, "I'm not going to speak to anyone I can't see." After a delay he slowly moved into the edge of the light, and I saw that he was—or had been, for his hair was now dark, and his accent had been lost—the rickshaw-puller known as Helmut.

"Was it not you who took me to the fireworks factory?"

"I was giving you enough rope," said he. "You see, it has been my conviction from the first that you came to our country with a favorable bias towards the Blonds. I was putting you to the test, and of course you failed—or rather, I should say you succeeded beautifully in confirming my theory."

"Why would I be favorably disposed to them when it was they who blew up my home in New York?"

He smiled sardonically. "Because cultured Americans adore those who abuse them in what is represented as a good cause."

"I assure you I am still happily enmired in the Me Generation," I cried with false enthusiasm. "I'm a monster of self-interest and have been denounced as such by a series of do-gooder women, for I am often attracted to social activists, if they have long legs and nice breasts." I was trying for a joke here, but without undue conviction that I would succeed. My lack of faith was appropriately rewarded: Helmut threatened to connect electrodes to my testicles and send a powerful current through them."

"You don't seem to understand," said he. "You're in the hands of the dreaded security police. You are dead to the outside world when you're in here, and vice versa. We can wash your brain like a handkerchief, flushing away your memories, hopes, ideals, and . . ." He searched for a word, did not find it, and murmuringly repeated "ideals." Aha! I thought, there's his usable weakness, a poor command of terms, but he soon confounded me by saying quickly, "And principles, values, convictions, and if I've left anything out with regard to the superego, you can be sure it will wash away as quickly as the rest."

"And you think my government will sit idly by while this is going on?"

"Certainly not," said he. "They'll launch nuclear missiles at us." His grin was unfunny. "Why, you poor schmuck!" he said, pretending to more compassion than he felt.

I decided to counterattack, though naturally in an extremely subtle way. "I think you're better-looking with blond hair."

He scowled. "Why should I care what you think?"

"I only just discovered that all Sebastianers are born blond."

His expression changed to one that might have been called uneasy. "That's common knowledge. We're all in the same boat to start with. Those who are content to stay there deserve to drown. Not much is asked, after all: just a little dye, but you see they're too lazy even for that."

"Not everyone is cut out to be blond all his life," I said, cunningly perverting his point, "but I think you could do it to advantage."

"Dammit," said Helmut.

"It's the shape of your jaw." I suggested a square with my fingers and thumbs.

I had got to him! He hung his head for a moment. "You might be right, but it's the political thing, you see. Were it simply aesthetics . . ." He showed a regretful pout.

"To be sure," I went on, "fair hair doesn't stay all that light on the adult head. So-called blond men usually have a head of dirty brown, if not snot-green."

He raised his chin further than required. "As you saw me with the rickshaw, that's entirely natural." He pointed at his scalp. "*This* is the dye-job."

"Then indeed you have beautiful hair."

He peered narrowly at me. "Are you a bugger after all?"

It was the "after all" that caught my interest. "Certainly not. I assume the concierge assured you of that truth. Does he not work for you?"

"Naturally," Helmut said. "Concierges are always police spies by tradition, as you very well know. Their mystique demands it. . . . Look, it's kind of you to admire my hair, but that doesn't alter the fact that we must force a confession out of you. I'm afraid that the means by which that will be done are extremely cruel. I say 'I'm afraid' merely to be courteous. Actually, I enjoy that phase of my job more than any other. I am that relatively rare person who is authorized to carry out his most outlandish fantasies in his everyday work."

"You do this in support of the status quo?"

"No," said Helmut. "I do it because I enjoy having the power to remove someone's freedom and to bring him pain."

"But you don't want to see the prince deposed?"

He shrugged. "I couldn't care less. My job is to ferret out dissenters and to frustrate their efforts. The means I employ represent my own interpretation of the work. I have infiltrated the liberation movement and can identify every one of its ringleaders. I could at any moment round all of them up and bring them here. But the fact is that, as you could see, they are a pack of harmless, ineffectual clowns here at home. Their bombs are used only in America. I would dearly like to torture them, enjoying the bringing of pain as I do, but alas! how can I do that when I already *know* all their secrets?"

"You can't do it to me, either," I said, rising from the chair. "Because before you can torture me, I confess!"

"Oh, no you don't!" he cried. "You cannot."

"But I have already done so, you see. Any torture you submit me to now would be contrary to the international standards of interrogation. You would reveal yourself as being a selfish sadist rather than a zealous investigator. Your authenticity would be shattered!"

Helmut threw his hands up. "All right, all right, you've made your point. But can't we just talk, at least?"

I had him on the run now. "Perhaps, if you'll just apologize for submitting me to this ordeal."

He spoke impatiently. "Consider it done. But your responsibility hasn't ended. What are you confessing *to?*"

"To being an American agent."

"OK. Now confess what sort of mischief you had planned to wreak in this role."

"None whatever. I'm on a fact-finding mission. But just a moment: Olga knew that. Why didn't you, if you have infiltrated the movement?"

He looked sheepish. "Well, all right, so I miss a few things. I don't get the rest I should, and I work darn hard, pulling that rickshaw, so I admit I catch a few winks whenever the opportunity offers itself. You don't know how boring it is to listen to revolutionary rhetoric. Another thing that limits the effectiveness of this agency is the lack of a name that can be used easily and gracefully, like Gestapo or KGB. It's awkward to pronounce the letter *S* five times in succession, and the term Five Esses, which we've tried to get people to use in recent years, simply doesn't sound serious."

I was still standing in the circle of light. "That's your problem," I said. "Having kept my end of the bargain, I'm leaving."

He clasped my arm and pleaded, "Look here, old fellow, can't you stay awhile? I could really use the company. You're someone I can talk to. This is a very lonely job. We might drink a beer or two and play some cards. I'll take you home for some of the best goulash you ever ate. Afterwards we'll listen to my brother-in-law play the concertina. And, say, my wife has another sister who's unmarried. You'll like her. She's—" He suggested, with cupped hands, a pair of enormous breasts, to carry which the woman would need a frame of the same kind.

He was about to resume when the door opened and one of the black-suited men came in.

"Sir," he said, "the revolution has begun."

"Of course it has," Helmut said derisively. "Led by that ridiculous Olga, no doubt."

"In fact, yes," said the man.

"I don't know why you've chosen this moment for your little joke, Stanislaus," said Helmut. "It's been a long day. Mr. Wren and I are going home now to a good dinner."

"It's not a joke, sir. The Blonds have taken the palace and captured the prince. Others are going around to all the government facilities. They'll be here at any moment. What shall we do, sir? Surrender or fight?"

"Hold them off until I wash this dye out of my hair!" cried Helmut, dashing for the door.

9

I ENCOUNTERED no one at all on my uncertain exit through the grim dark passageways of the building of the SSSSS (a name easier to write than to speak). When I finally emerged I had no idea of where I might be. However, when I rounded the first corner, I saw The Linden Street School at the end of the street. I had been only a block from where the security people had picked me up, and it was a short walk from there to the hotel.

As I passed the school I glanced through the glass-paneled front doors and saw that the audience was once again entering the auditorium from the hall or lobby. It would seem as if news of the revolution had not yet reached them—or they were simply indifferent to it.

But changes had already been made at the hotel. For one, its name, according to the replaced brass plate on either side of the entrance, was now The Hotel Blond. I was confronted by the concierge, whose hair was now a mass of tight yellow curls and who had exchanged his tailcoat for a resplendent uniform tunic, draped with braid and bearing an embroidered legend on the left breast: again "The Hotel Blond." I suspected that he had not only been the classic concierge in serving as police spy, but had typified the traditional police spy by being a double agent.

"Halt!" he cried from behind the desk. "Your identification!"

"Come off it."

He flushed and brought, from under the counter, the Luger he had drawn on me once before, then with his free hand he banged the little domed bell before him. In a moment the bellboy appeared, the same whose flesh he had tried to sell me on numerous occasions. The concierge ordered him to search my person, which the lad proceeded to do, and though presumably a catamite he was discreet enough with his hands. He wore the old uniform with a newly embroidered Hotel Blond breast patch.

Next the concierge lifted the telephone and tried to reach the police but had no success. Lowering the instrument, he spoke to me as if I might be sympathetic.

"I suppose we must be patient. The changeover is not quite complete."

I asked sourly, "What are you charging me with this time?"

"Refusal to identify yourself to an officer."

"You're an officer?"

"Do you not see my uniform?"

"It's the costume of a hotel flunky!" I cried. "Whom are you trying to fool?"

"I'm afraid your troubles are growing," he said with false regret. "*Everybody* in any kind of uniform is perforce an officer of the Revolution. It is a grave offense to insult one of us."

"Just a moment. A mailman is an officer?"

"Certainly. As is a nurse." He moved his heavy head from side to side. I suspected that though obviously he had been prepared with clothing and signplates, the Revolution had caught him with insufficient time in which to bleach his dark-dyed hair and that that which crowned his skull was a wig.

"This bellboy wears a uniform!" I pointed out.

"And he's an officer," shouted the concierge.

"Do you admit that the last time I saw you, a scant few hours ago, you showed quite another attitude towards the Blonds?"

He addressed the lad, who had withdrawn from me. "Lieutenant, what was consistently my position on the Blonds when they were a despised and oppressed minority?"

The boy clicked his heels. "Sir, you always admired them and in so doing took an enormous risk."

"There you are," the concierge said smugly.

I grimaced. "Your effrontery is breathtaking. As to the 'lieutenant' here, how recently was it that you were trying to peddle him for sexual purposes?"

"Oho." The large man moaned in pleasurable anticipation. "I wouldn't want to be in your shoes when I get hold of the police!

Sexual inversion is of course counterrevolutionary, as is indecency with respect to a minor. The lieutenant is but seventeen years old. To have made importunities to him is the foulest of crimes. . . . Indeed, you are such a heinous criminal, all in all, that I am justified, as a colonel in the Revolutionary Blond Army, to sentence you to death on my own authority." He raised the Luger to point at my head. It might have been a bluff, as so many things proved to be in Saint Sebastian, but I was not inclined to put him to the test.

Fortunately, I did not have to, for Clyde McCoy reeled into the lobby at that moment, leaned across the counter and disarmed the concierge, and spoke to me.

"*There* you are. I've been lookin' for you, sport. Thought you might have located a source for something to drink by now."

"You haven't heard of the revolution?"

"Huh? Oh, that. That's *their* business."

"What will become of the prince, do you think?"

McCoy shrugged. "They'll probably knock him off." He took the clip from the Luger and returned the weapon to the concierge, who smiled obsequiously and thanked him. The bellhop had disappeared.

"You are curiously unimpressed," I told the veteran correspondent. "You don't expect your own status to be altered?"

McCoy gave me his bleary eye. "I took the poet's advice many years ago and abandoned excessive expectation about anything. That philosophy has left me untouched by human hands, if you know what I mean."

"But with all respect, McCoy, is that any way to live?"

He groaned. "You call this living? I haven't had a drink for an hour!"

"The Blonds have closed the wine shops and taverns?"

He squinted at me. "Is *that* the reason? I thought they just ran out of goods, which happens a lot. The distillery breaks down." He turned and lurched towards the door. "Come on."

In truth, I had nothing better to do, not to mention that in such a time I felt secure in McCoy's presence, the drunk tending to enjoy the status of a holy idiot in most cultures or anyway someone who is given a wide berth (except on the iconoclastic pavements of the Big Apple, where he might well be set on fire).

I followed McCoy out to his car and was about to take my chances with the passenger's door when he directed me to enter by way of the window. I did so, sliding headfirst through the aperture, then falling inside. Meanwhile he inserted himself behind the steering wheel, and soon we were roaring and rattling up the hills towards the palace.

When I saw what our destination would be, I asked, "You think it's the opportune time to go there?"

"Damn right," said McCoy, setting his jaw. "I'm not going to let them get away with this Prohibition shit."

"You can stop them?"

He scowled at the windshield. "I'm an American, for Christ sake."

It was so strange nowadays to hear the term used in that way —though it was no doubt routine in the movies shown by the priest.

We gained the summit and shortly thereafter scraped to a stop against the wall overlooking the moat. We left the car and climbed the spiral staircase in the tower. The old journalist displayed an impressive spryness. No doubt he was energized by the expectation of getting a drink from the stores of the deposed monarch.

When we reached those corridors through which I had been conducted by General Popescu on my previous visit to the palace, I saw that the walls had been denuded of the so-called Old Masters.

We still had not seen a Blond, or, for that matter, anyone from the ancien régime, but when we finally reached the first of what had formerly been the sumptuously furnished antechambers to the throne room but now was empty except for a desk of gray metal, atop and around which were a number of matching accessories, intercom, wastecan, telephone, there sat a young fair-haired woman. She wore a suit of some gray material with a slight sheen, a white blouse, and a black bow tie. Her hair was pulled into a tight bun at her nape. She was wearing no jewelry and no makeup.

I had assumed that McCoy would continue and perhaps even intensify the truculence with which he had greeted my suggestion that the new leaders were teetotallers, but in fact he now turned on an old-fashioned charm, or in any event, what he obviously intended to be taken as such.

"Sweetie," he crooned, so to speak quasimodoing his body, lowering his head to leer on the level of her own, "Could I ask you kindly to let me see Who's in Charge?"

She nodded crisply and bent over a chart that lay flat on the desk pad. She stabbed at a certain place with the eraser of an unsharpened pencil. "I can give you five oh five P.M., Wednesday the twenty-fourth."

"Honey," said McCoy, "that's next week."

"It's next month."

"Now, darling," said the veteran newsman, "I'm Clyde McCoy, pool correspondent for a number of important American wire services and TV and radio networks. I'm *sure* you folks would want me to give you a good send-off in the dispatches I send back to the States."

"One moment, sir," said the receptionist, and she threw a switch on the intercom and spoke into it so rapidly that I could not grasp a word. She was answered with a grunt.

She nodded. "You may proceed."

"Thank you, snookums," said McCoy, and we opened the door behind her and entered the next room. This was another of the chambers that had been hung with the royal collection of bogus paintings. Like the one we had just left, it was now furnished only with a metal desk. Behind this one sat a young man dressed in a suit of the same material as that of the girl next door, a white shirt, and a black bow tie. He was ex-Lieutenant Blok, of the old palace guard, the officer who had strip-searched me just that morning. His hair was now blond.

He asked brightly, with a touch of arrogance, "May I help you?"

McCoy used another style this time. He swaggered up and rested one buttock on the edge of the desk. "Maybe you can, sonny-boy, maybe you just can. I wanna see the Big Fellow."

"And who would that—"

But McCoy interrupted with a pointing finger. "Just call me through, junior, and I won't report you for having pecker tracks on your fly." He winked, got up, and did not bother to wait for

Blok to execute the orders; the latter at the moment was conducting an anxious inspection of his trousers.

In the third room, the last of the antechambers, was an exceptionally large and husky man, whose blond hair was clipped close to his outsized skull. He looked uncomfortable in the gray suit and black bow tie and out of place at a desk.

He asked, in the hostility-tinged though technically neutral voice of a professional in the craft of bringing people to, or keeping them in, order, "What do you fellows want?"

The versatile McCoy made another change of tone or tune. He barked, "You call this security?"

The big man's eyes lost half their diameter. "What do *you* call it?"

"Swiss cheese," said the journalist. He pulled a pen from an inside pocket of his wretched jacket and pointed it at the large Blond. "If this was a gun, you'd be a memory."

"Yeah, but you wouldn't get any further unless I pressed this button," the large man said, reaching under the desktop.

McCoy found a piece of paper in his breast pocket and unfolded it. "All right. That'll go in my report."

"Report?"

"He and I are doing a security check," said McCoy, nodding at me. "You just squeak through—unless I decide otherwise." He put the paper onto the desk and scribbled on it. "Now hit the button."

The big man did as asked. One of the double doors swung open, and we passed into what had formerly been the throne room of Sebastian XXIII.

Now the long chamber was in the process of being subdivided, like one of those contemporary office floors, by the introduction of standing panels of opaque corrugated plastic. An army of carpenters was so occupied. Meanwhile desks were in place, in a regular pattern throughout the vast room, and gray-suited Blond functionaries were already seated at them. Every one at whom I looked was speaking on the telephone, perhaps to a colleague in the same room, for when one hung up, the rest of them did the same. The throne was gone, as was even the dais on which it had stood. The entire corps of gray suits was now, simultaneously, stapling sheaves of paper.

I stopped at one desk and asked, "Where's Olga?"

"Olga who?" The young woman continued to use the stapler.

"Then who's in charge?"

"Of which department?"

"The whole country."

"I'm sorry, sir," said she. "That's not my job."

I started to leave, but on second thought tarried to ask, "What *is* your job?"

She put a finger to her cheek. "I haven't been told yet. I was just hired."

"At the end of the day?" I asked. "Without warning? I see a movie, and when I come out, a revolution has occurred?"

She gave me a sympathetic sad smile. "I don't know about that. But as my old teacher, Sister Thérèse, used to say, 'In the movies you lose all track of time, don't you?' "

I left her. It was then that I observed that McCoy was no longer in the vicinity. I scanned the area but saw only gray suits and workmen carrying panels of corrugated plastic.

I left the throne room and went through more barren halls, looked into more chambers, and saw more gray desks and people who, except for their hair, matched them, and now computer terminals were beginning to appear on the desktops, but I did not encounter anyone from the ruling group of Blonds whom I had met in the subterranean room at the fireworks factory. To the naked eye this revolution looked as though it had succeeded only in transforming the palace into a branch of IBM.

Finally, in one of the marble corridors I met someone I recognized: Popescu, now apparently an ex-general, for he was wearing coveralls and pushing a longhandled broom.

I had no wish to embarrass him, but I was desperate for news as to what had taken place. "General," I said, "I—"

Tears sprang from his eyes. He dropped his broom and embraced me. "You *remembered!* Oh, how kind!"

"It was only this morning," I said. I stepped back: he stank of sweat. "Was there much fighting? Did you resist? Is the prince dead?"

Popescu shrugged. "It was astonishingly quick. It happened after lunch, when we were all taking our siestas."

"But the palace guard?"

"Undoubtedly there would have been bloodshed had they been attacked with routine weapons, but you could well imagine how terrifying it was to confront an invasion of movingmen carrying metal office furniture and computer equipment, followed by one shock wave after another of clerks wearing vulgar lounge suits cut from synthetic stuff, and black bow ties."

"The prince was captured?"

"One assumes so," said the ex-general. "One is reluctant to ask too many questions. I trust I won't be harmed if I do a good job at this." He brandished his broom and even managed a smile.

"Would you know a big Blond named Olga?"

He shook his head.

"She was the leader of the liberation movement."

"I'm afraid I've never heard of it."

With some impatience I said, "They're the people who made the revolution. You know, the Blonds."

"Not this revolution, with all respect."

"But all the people working here have fair hair."

"Indeed. As everyone knows, Blonds make the best bureaucrats. They have the sort of docile temperament that is ideal in such a situation, and are especially good at such routine tasks as using the telephone, the Wheeldex, and the computer terminal."

"Then who *did* lead the takeover? Who's the boss now?"

"Gregor."

"Who in the world *is* he?"

"He's the man in charge," Popescu said curtly, and began to apply his broom to the floor between us. "He'd not be likely to notice anyone in my lowly position: at least, I pray he won't." He gave me a fearful wince and moved on.

"But I'm an American," I cried. "Where can I find him?"

He told me which turns to make, then returned to sweeping the floor he had lately strode in polished boots. I followed his directions, arriving at last at a suite of interconnecting rooms, the last of which was made, walls, floor, and the stupendously large bathtub embedded in the latter, of white marble with prominent blue veins.

An obese body was lowering itself into the tub as I entered. Obviously these were the royal quarters, and the prince was quite OK, though apparently not attended by any of his former people or anyone else.

"Your Royal Highness!" I began to apologize.

But I had had a rear view. When the huge rump had disappeared below the surface of the water, followed by half the massive block of flesh that formed his back—the oversized tub must have been a yard deep—the head turned and the profile I saw was not that of Prince Sebastian but rather that of my acquaintance from the Hotel Bristol, the enormous and silent but affable lover of Caruso and pesto!

He now spoke for the first time. "Meester Ran. Please to take seat." He gestured at a scroll-armed bench, a kind of Roman thing, against the nearest marble wall. His accent was not Italian.

I did as asked and said, "You are Gregor?"

His body made a movement that caused the water to be agitated briefly. "And you," he asked, "are from the Firm?"

I neither confirmed nor denied this as he found a sponge and a cake of soap in niches in the tub above the waterline, and began to abrade one against the other.

Instead I asked, "I am told that you are running this thing."

He made a moue. "I halp Sebastiani pipples."

"The Blonds?"

"Bluns, everybody." He had worked up a supply of lather sufficiently generous to hide his hands.

"But you are not yourself a Sebastianer."

"Nor you," said he.

"That's true, but I haven't made a revolution."

He began to soap his shoulders and hairy upper chest with the lather-laden sponge. "Not ravolution, but improved efficiency."

"What have you done with the prince?"

"He laft."

"Where was he taken?"

Gregor began to work soap into the thick black hair atop his head. "Wherever he wants."

"Who are you?" I asked.

"Gregor," said he. He left his soapy scalp to pick up the floating sponge and push it in my direction. "Wash my beck."

I rose abruptly, but rather to show my resentment than to

obey his command. "While the liberation movement was playing its naïve little game, you simply walked in and took over the country, didn't you? But what I want to know is, *why?* Surely you must have seen that it is a place of no consequence in the greater scheme of things."

He smiled broadly, displaying the gold teeth at either end of his dental range. "*You* was going to." He shook the sponge at me again. "Scrob my beck!"

"The joke's on you," I said. "I was just about to make my final report that the place is worthless. You've got a white elephant on your hands. Don't you know that nobody works? Most of the populace spends its days at the movies, and the economy runs on credit. The country's too small to be of strategic value and has no useful raw materials. What can you use it for?"

"Example of democracy in action," said he. He gave me a stare of some duration, then whistled and in a moment and from nowhere appeared three stocky men with the faces of plug-uglies. They stood glowering at me. They were not Blonds. They were much more formidable-looking than the old black-suited secret police of Helmut's.

I went to the tub, crouched on the marble floor, and accepted the sponge, which under the circumstances felt slimy but probably was not literally so, and did as ordered. He had quite a growth of hair on his shoulder blades.

"Is that sufficient?" I asked after I had scrubbed for a while.

"Sure," said Gregor.

I returned the sponge to him and got to my feet.

"See," he said, grinning up at me. "I ain't so bed a guy! At least you din't never have to wash my balls!" He laughed so heartily that he almost lowered his face into the lathered water. When he recovered his breath he said, "So you can go in peace, Ran. Sebastiani Airline got a night flight leaves one hour. So long and have a nice day."

"I'm being expelled?"

"I don't believe you was ever here, you know?" Gregor said, not unkindly. As one might say, he was only doing his job.

"Well, obviously you've won," I said, "though I'm not sure how or what. Do you intend to put a lot of people to death as counterrevolutionaries?"

He smirked. "You got crazy ideas. We ain't going kill anybody. Put them to work on public projects! Make life better for pipples."

"What kind of work?"

"Farmss."

"Huh." I tweaked my chin. "I never thought about it—there's a New Yorker for you—but obviously they must have some domestic sources for food, since I was told they didn't import much."

"Nice farmss beyond airport," said Gregor. "All the way to the base of mountains, and farmers work hard, don't sit in movies all day. We make more farmers."

This was beginning to make sense. "And if you grow a surplus of food, you'll export it, no doubt?"

Gregor rose dripping from the tub. He had a remarkable body, fat but not soft; perhaps when younger he had been one of the super-heavyweight power-lifters for which his culture was famous. I half expected him to order me to give him a toweling, but I was wrong. He had a nice sense of proportion; he had already made his humiliating point.

He answered my question. "They don't need all the food they got. They going to plant flowers."

"I'll be damned. You're not going aesthetic, are you, Gregor?"

"Poppies," said he, with a slow smug smile.

I was even more damned now, but I did not say so. Instead I chuckled humorlessly. "I didn't know you guys use the stuff."

"Not us," said Gregor. "But *you* sure as shit will!" Now his laughter was so violent as to shake his vast body, watching which was as if to await an eruption of Mount Saint Helens. The marble room continued to ring for some time after he had stopped. His bravos were slow to join him in mirth, no doubt because they were deficient in English, but one of them brought him a towel.

Unfortunately I had no rejoinder, expecting as I did that the Western world would end not with a whimper but a fix. I changed the subject. "Mind telling me what became of Sebastian's collection of art?"

"Confiscated," Gregor answered. "Is nawt right for one man to have all expensive stuff. Give to pipples." He spread wide his treetrunk legs and went between them and under the great projection of his belly to dry his crotch, vigorously tumbling his genitals in a towel.

"But which people?"

"Hell's bells," said he. "We are all pipples, ain't we?"

He did not seem to be aware that the artworks were counterfeit. It was my one pitiful score off him and secret at that, but it was a point on which to leave.

"Good-bye, Gregor. I can't say it's been a pleasure, though to be courteous I suppose I should thank you for the pesto. Where'd you learn to make that?"

"Travel lots of places," said he, gesturing. "Gosh, I like to pick up some culture. Food! Opera!" He abraded his breech with the towel. "See you next place, Ran."

"Only in the funny papers, Gregor," said I. "I'm not a pro at this. I know it'll give you only more contempt for me to hear it, but I'm essentially a playwright."

He was drying his armpits. "Hey," he cried, "you could stay here and write some plays."

My chance had come at last! Who knows what might have become of me had he not added, "Nice plays to show pipples how to behave themselves."

"Pity," I said, "but my work is the degenerate stuff that would have just the opposite effect: Manhattan slice-of-life, characters who pay two-thirds of their income for an uncomfortable apartment and the remainder to a psychiatrist, who forsake parents, spouses, close friends, to search for someone who can *really* love them."

He put a twist of towel into one ear socket. "Be good for bad examples."

"I doubt it. See, I make them sympathetic. I'm afraid I would be a subversive element."

He scowled at me. "In all the world, only an American would boast of that."

"Then maybe there's still some slight hope for us." I left before he could change his mind.

10

IN MY EAGERNESS to leave the palace I forgot about McCoy and remembered him again only when I saw his car just across the drawbridge. He was sitting behind the wheel, drinking from the neck of a magnum.

He grimaced at me as I slithered into the car via the window. "This was all that's left. They already poured out most of the old brandy and other spirits. They got gangs at work on that, at the drains of the royal laundry. Fucking barbarians!"

"I'm supposed to leave the country on the next plane," I told him. "You'd better come along."

He let some more wine run down his throat and made a pickleface. He handed the bottle to me. "Did this go bad? Taste it."

I did as asked, then looked at the label: it was the legendary Romanée-Conti, the biggest of the reds, too costly for anyone but reigning monarchs, sitcom stars, and defense counsel for the downtrodden. "It's just too good for you, McCoy. What about leaving Saint Sebastian?"

He reclaimed the bottle. "God, I don't know. And leave everything I've built up over the years?"

"Which is what? A crummy hotel room?"

"Shit, I'm not ready to go Stateside just yet."

"It's been forty years since that war ended!"

He gulped some more wine. "I wonder if *Time* or the AP could use a Continental smut correspondent on a regular basis?"

"You could always ask," I said. "But let's get going. I'm supposed to catch the plane within an hour." I told him about Gregor.

"One of the things I'd miss is this old bucket of bolts. I hear they got all-metal station wagons now—?"

"Yes, I think since before I was born. No doubt you'll find everything has been changed since you left, but the same is probably true of every other place. I hear Paris and London have been stacked with glass skyscrapers since I was there on summer vacation, via Icelandic Airlines, less than twenty years ago." McCoy's presence brought out the nostalgia in me.

"Jesus," he said. "If I went home I might be spotted by the old lady or one of the kids."

"You've got a family? Your children would be older than I!"

He took the bottle from his mouth and swallowed loudly. "You know how it is. They been taken care of. Military allotment."

"Wouldn't that have ended years ago?"

"But they got the GI insurance, I'm sure. Just before I went over the hill from Germany to here, see, I found a dead Nazi of the right size, hung my dog tags around his neck, and dressed him in my uniform. The ball-'n'-chain would've got ten grand. That was real mazooma in those days."

"You could avoid her part of the country. But I think it's imperative that you get away from here. Gregor and Company aren't your kind of people, McCoy. You see what they've done with the prince's cellarful of drinkables, and I hardly think they'll look kindly on the sort of writing you do. Let's head right for the airport."

"I have to stop by the hotel and pick up my stuff," said he, hurling the now empty bottle from the window and starting up the catarrhal engine.

We hurtled downhill. When we reached the bottom we proceeded to pass most of the places with which I had had some association during my short time in Saint Sebastian. Already these had been altered or were in the process of changing. Of the open-air markets, only a stall selling potatoes was open for business. The birds had disappeared, along with the fake fish and the fishwives. The pillory was gone from the square, and a number of workmen were erecting a scaffold that looked ominously as if it might well become a gallows. A cul-de-sac that greatly resembled the old Street of Words was now signposted as Truth Lane. At the moment the pavement in front of the writers' pink building was being scrubbed, with soap and brush, on hands and knees, by what looked from my distance like some of the authors I had met, Spang, Boggs, and poor sybaritic Riesling, provoking whom I now regretted.

When we reached the hotel a Blond functionary, in gray suit and black tie, was behind the desk.

"Mr. Wren," said he, and handed me an envelope he had taken from one of the pigeonholes behind him.

It was a cablegram from Langley, VA.

NOBODY NAMED RASMUSSEN AT
THIS ADDRESS, AND NOTHING
CALLED THE FIRM. BE ADVISED
IT IS ILLEGAL TO IMPERSONATE
AN EMPLOYEE OF A FEDERAL AGENCY.
THE COMPANY

This was Rasmussen's idea of a joke.

I peered at the man behind the desk. "Aren't you Helmut?"

"Formerly. I've made a successful transition. Of course, I would have liked to be a secret policeman for the new regime, but I failed to pass the entrance exam."

"A difficult test?"

"Yes. I was supposed to throttle one of my old colleagues with my bare hands."

I shudderingly changed the subject. "You did a good job in washing the dye from your hair, unless that's a wig. Which reminds me: what became of the old concierge?"

"Transferred."

So despite his desperate efforts to climb onto the revolutionary bandwagon the fat opportunist had not been able to save himself.

"Do you now manage the hotel?"

"No, sir. I simply work here. One of Mr. Gregor's associates is in charge. Do you wish to see him?"

Helmut made a swift movement below the counter and brought up a sheet of paper. "Your bill, sir."

This was one obligation I could scan with a light heart. "Haha! I see you charged me two hundred dollars a day. I'd certainly object, if I actually had to pay that, for I have merely shared the room in which Mr. McCoy lives permanently, which is not even equipped with a bathroom, nor with twin beds. Not to mention that I haven't stayed overnight in it. And then, haha, I would scarcely be paying you in US currency."

Helmut's expression remained impassive. "But you're leaving the country, sir. I'm afraid your credit is effective only while you remain here, and we have no currency of our own."

"Well, I don't have two hundred dollars."

Helmut smiled sadly. "If you will notice, the meals make it a bit more."

I had quickly glanced at only the first line of the bill. I now raised it for a more careful study and saw the following itemization:

Café complet, Sebastiani Airlines		$ 15.00
Lunch at Palace	(prix fixe)	65.00
	champagne	110.00
Late lunch, House of Authors	(visitor's rate)	45.00
Pesto & jug wine		35.00
Movie *(Gats 'n' Gals)*		7.50
	subtotal	277.50
	service	41.63
	value added tax	27.75
	NYC sales tax	23.59
	Total room & board	570.47
	Revolutionary surtax	57.05
	Grand Total	$627.52

"I don't know where I should begin," I said, with the overwhelming sense of defeat I get when outrage exceeds a certain limit (this of course was a daily phenomenon on the city streets). "Perhaps by simply pointing out that charge which is among the least in money but the most heinous in its moral status, namely, New York City sales tax. I'm here, not there."

Helmut said patiently, "But you're *from* there."

"Look, Gregor has asked me to leave the country. That, conjoined with the fact that I have no money whatever, should be enough to close the discussion."

"Oh, I *am* sorry," said Helmut, "but it was Gregor himself

who just phoned me to ask that I be sure to collect payment from you before you left. I'll have to call the manager."

He depressed a new bell push that had been installed at the edge of the desk, and in a trice a thickset man, with heavy eyebrows and a forehead that began an inch above them, came through a rear door and glowered at me.

Fortunately McCoy returned at the same moment, stepping off the elevator with a faded green duffle bag in one hand and my suitcase in the other. "I brought your shit, too," said he.

"Oh, I didn't wan—" I caught myself and, taking the valise from him, turned to the new manager of the Bristol Hotel. "I don't have the money for the bill," I said, "but as a man of your sophistication must surely know, it is traditional in such cases for the hostelry to confiscate the luggage." I put the suitcase on the countertop and opened it. Quickly extracting the knitted shirt and old cords, which McCoy had thoughtfully included, I said, "Here's an entire wardrobe for travel, in the most fashionable American colors, every item guaranteed to be of a synthetic material that will look new eternally." I began to disrobe and add the items I had been wearing to the collection, and I donned the clothes in which I had been shanghaied.

I had finally made a sound judgment. An expression of delight came over the simian features of the manager as he inspected the gaudy garments, the madras jacket, the plastic shoes, the Day-Glo socks, etc.

He grunted his assent, and McCoy and I left the hotel. The veteran journalist was subdued and drove to the airport with none of his usual verve.

As opposed to the informality in which I had landed, we were now obliged to run the gantlet of a number of Blond functionaries in gray suits, with an occasional glimpse of one of the thugs imported by Gregor. An exit visa was waiting for me, but it had to be examined and stamped by one official after another in the terminal building, and when that process was finally completed, I was taken into a lavatory and forced to undergo a humiliating spread-cheek strip search, more thorough than that conducted by Blok: this one was managed by a Gregorian wearing a rubber glove.

McCoy, for whom no exit permit was ready, had been separated from me and taken elsewhere in the terminal. Under the old regime he would not have suffered this ordeal of red tape, but he was displaying a new docility. When he had not reappeared by the time I was finally ready to be led out to the airplane, I protested. The gray suits appealed, in what had apparently been established as the line of command, to the nearest of Gregor's men, and the latter's continuous brow came down over his small eyes as he drew a wicked-looking sap from his back pocket and raised it to strike me.

But McCoy saved me one more time, reappearing from a door near at hand and, in the imperious style of old, shouting at the secret policeman. The man was startled, but no doubt hearing what he took as the note of authentic authority, he complied.

To me the vintage newsman said, "Look, Wren, I've just had a phone talk with Gregor. He can use my professional skills, as it happens. He offered me the job of Minister of Information. I'll be writing about the achievements of the revolution."

My expression must have reflected my thoughts.

"I don't care what you want to call it," McCoy said defensively. "I'm too old to go back to the States at this late date. This is a good job. Turns out that though Prohibition will be in effect for most of the population—except on certain holidays honoring phases of the revolution—you can drink all you want if you're an insider."

"Do you realize what you're going to have to write?"

He let his mouth droop on one side, presumably to indicate wryness. "Piece of cake."

Suddenly I saw the light. "It was *your* idea, wasn't it? How'd you talk Gregor into it?"

"Hell, man, I'm an old pro! I assured him that in the dispatches I sent out to the world I would naturally fail to mention any atrocities committed by his crowd while exaggerating or inventing altogether the vicious outrages of the opposition, if there was any opposition: if there wasn't, I'd invent one. Were he to find it necessary to massacre people en masse, I would present such events as counterattacks against forces that far outnumbered his own small band of gallant freedom fighters. I assured him I could also be counted on to honor the principle of revolutionary modesty and denounce the cult of personality, exalting only those members of the prevailing power elite and expunging the names of persons who, despite their contributions, had been outmaneuvered by their comrades."

I realized I had underestimated the old fellow, but did wonder why he had wasted so many years at sex-reportage and not the kind that had a greater sway amongst persons of culture.

"All right, McCoy. Though much younger than you, I'm already too old for expressions of moral indignation."

"Fuck you too, Wren," said he, but rather blithely, without spite.

Two of the gray suits led me out onto the field where the airplane, a propeller-driven craft reminiscent of the old Icelandic machinery, was waiting. I climbed the steps, entered the cabin, and saw several recognizable persons.

I greeted the stewardess, who was back in the old familiar abbreviated uniform. "Back at your post, I see, Olga."

She gave me the synthetic smile of the profession and the ritualistic welcome-on-board, then went forward, to the cockpit, with a trayful of coffee and cups.

I moved along the aisle to my favorite midship area and said good day to my nearby fellow passengers, the ex-concierge of the Hotel Bristol and the catamite bellhop for whom he had served as ponce. They were both now in subdued mufti.

I did not expect the man to be embarrassed, and he was not. "Well, Mr. Wren," said he, "soon we'll all be making our fortunes in New York."

"Frankly," I said, not without a tinge of bitterness, "I expect you will be quite at home there in no time."

"Yes," said he, hovering on the verge of a smug simper, "I've been offered a position as maître d'hôtel at Les Cinq Lettres." This was one of Manhattan's most expensive and therefore most publicized eateries, visited at least once a year by the human-interest reporter on each TV channel's news team, who ordered a conspicuously *nouvelle* dish—say, sea urchins on artichoke pasta, blueberry-vinaigrette sauce—and was wry about the astronomical price.

"And him?" I indicated the former bellboy.

"My son," said the concierge, "has been hired by Mr. Rasmussen for his male burlesque theater."

"Your son . . . Rasmussen . . ." The astonishments continued to be greater as the sequence proceeded, for at that moment the man himself, Rasmussen in the flesh, emerged from one of the forward toilets. He had coarsely saved the zipping of his fly as an exhibit for his fellow passengers.

"Rasmussen!" I cried, going up the aisle. "You—"

He looked up from his crotch. "Wren! The very man I wanted to see. I just flew in, and I'm flying right back out with this load of Sebastiani boat people." His complexion was as bad as I remembered.

"Are you or are you not CIA?"

"I never said we were. I always said Firm, not Company."

"Then what's the Firm?"

"Private enterprise, babe."

"Don't call me babe. You've used me, you've taken advantage of my patriotic feelings."

"The term you're looking for is 'jerked off,' I believe," he said grinning. "Actually, if you were really patriotic, you ought to commend me."

"For what?"

"What do you think, you dork? For bringing Saint Sebastian into the democratic camp."

"Gregor is a totalitarian!"

"I don't mean that shit," Rasmussen said, rubbing some dandruff from his sandy hair. "I'm selling them a lot of seconds in stereo equipment, surplus canned goods, recalled models of certain cars, and, hey, can you beat this: a big stock of Nehru jackets, in storage in Jersey for fifteen years. And you helped. You oughta feel some pride."

"Oh, yeah? Well, I'll expose you, Rasmussen! There are investigative reporters who would kill for such a story as I can give them."

He laughed negligently. "You're welcome to try, but I think most of the media are in my pocket. See, we got the big star. Prince Sebastian signed an exclusive contract with us."

"Sebastian the Twenty-third?"

"Of course. I already got him booked with dinner theaters, women's-rights organizations, and self-realization groups across the country."

"Then he's been allowed to leave here?"

"It's part of my package deal with Gregor and Company."

"So you're a talent agency?"

"Among other things. We're a conglomerate, babe."

No doubt they published *Crotch*, the paper for which McCoy had been foreign correspondent, as well. I didn't ask. I was still seething. But there was nothing I could do about my hunger for revenge until we reached home, and frankly I had my doubts as to what I could do even then, for Rasmussen was obviously much closer to the ruthless center of the New York mainstream than I was likely ever to be. He could even afford to eat in such restaurants as the one in which the concierge would be maître d'. And he also could hold his own with the likes of Gregor. The people who know how to handle themselves seem to be similar, irrespective of ideology.

"I assume it was you who got him"—I indicated the former concierge—"his new job. Well, then, I—"

Rasmussen interrupted. "Isn't he the *perfect* mater? Subservient to a clique of the initiates, yet mercilessly abusive to the humble stranger who wanders onto the premises under the erroneous impression that it is a foddering place."

"What I was going to say was, if you would render such aid to a foreigner, perhaps you'd do a favor for a fellow American whose life you've disrupted in the interests of a commercial scheme of questionable morality. I don't suppose any of your enterprises are involved with the theater?"

"Why, they certainly are!" said he. "We bring a lot of shows to Broadway."

"Broadway? You don't mean it!" One's opportunities come in the most bizarre ways. What a grueling experience I had had to undergo to meet a producer at last!

"I don't know whether I've mentioned this, but I am essentially a playwright."

Rasmussen leaned very close to me and poked me in the chest with a rigid forefinger. "Let me tell you something, Wren: so is everybody."

I had briefly become obsequious, but I bridled now. "You bastard you! You owe me something."

He took a step back, and his eyes widened to show even more

discolor. "Where'd you get the spunk all of a sudden? I like that, Wren. It'll take you farther than that habitual bitterness of yours. Read your Nietzsche and you'll find that all the world's ills can be traced to *ressentiment.*" He reached into an interior pocket and brought out a rectangle of pasteboard. "Bring your stuff up to the office when we get back. I can't promise you more than a reading, but I'll tell you this: it'll be read by somebody who's fluent in English."

He gave me the card, which proved to be something called American Cousin Productions, with an address in Shubert Alley.

Not wishing to be near the concierge, I took a seat up front, but had not sat there long when Olga emerged from the cockpit with her tray. When she reached my row she stopped and said coldly, "I'm sorry, sir, but this is the First Class section."

"I'm being ejected from the country," I said. "*Your* country, which has just had a revolution in which you, the leader of the liberation movement, obviously played no part. And which has left you in the same position as before."

"At least I don't have to pretend to be a cretin any more," said she, with what I must admit was a certain dignity. "Now, unless you can produce a First Class ticket, you must return to the Tourist section."

"I don't have a ticket of any kind."

"But if you *did* have one," she said stubbornly, "it would be Economy."

I sullenly got up and she moved on. Farther along the aisle I encountered another familiar face: that of the cable clerk.

"Yes," he said, before I could speak, "I'm exiling myself while it's still possible. I'm heading for Hollywood. I want to take a tour of the stars' homes, see where some of my favorites live: Ginny Simms, Gloria Jean, Bob Burns: I love to hear him play the bazooka."

"A forward-looking project," said I. "But did you know that your former sovereign is soon to become a popular lecturer in America?"

"That big palooka will take the cake!" the clerk told me enthusiastically. "He's triple threat. Call him anything but late for breakfast. Who you think's flying this egg-crate?"

It took me more than a moment to get any sense out of this mishmash of outmoded jargon. Then: "You're saying the prince is our *pilot?*"

"You ain't just bumping your gums together. It's ceiling zero, visibility zero, and we're comin' in on a wing and a prayer."

As he spoke it came to my attention that the aircraft had begun to move: I had been subliminally aware that the engines had been idling for some time. Olga came along and insisted I take a seat and fasten the belt, and then upbraided me for putting a suitcase in the overhead rack.

"It's not mine!"

"A likely story," said she, and demanded that I put it under the seat in front of me; if it didn't fit, the takeoff would be delayed while the case was ejected.

"It's yours, isn't it?" I angrily asked the cable clerk, across the aisle.

"Not on your tintype," said he. He moved his head to indicate the ex-concierge. "Belongs to that hepcat."

Therefore I did as ordered. The case must have contained stolen metallic things from the hotel, clinking and heavy as it was, and I had the greatest difficulty in moving it with no aid from anybody. But when it was lowered, it did fit under the seat.

"Now," said Olga, scowling down at me, "extinguish your cigar, cigarette, or pipe."

"As you can see," I said derisively, "I'm not smoking."

She brought a pack of cigarettes from the pocket of her tunic. "Take one of these and light it." She gave me a cigarette and a folder of matches, and actually forced me to take a puff or two, again threatening to stop the aircraft unless I complied.

I obeyed her, but I did demand an explanation.

"It is one of the new regulations of the People's Airline," said she. "Gregor has warned us that the punishment will be stern for any failure to enforce any rule. Since nobody on this flight was smoking, it was impossible to observe the regulation. You were the obvious choice to bring about the proper state of affairs. Now put the cigarette out, so that we might take off promptly."

The takeoff, when it came, seemed professional enough.

When the plane was level again, the intercom came on in a rush of static, and someone, presumably Prince Sebastian, said something through the auditory fog, but as on every flight I have taken throughout my life, only the odd word was comprehensible. I gather our altitude was specified in thousands, and the phrase "on your left" would suggest that the passengers were urged to look out those windows for a view of something on the ground.

That the ex-sovereign of the country was now piloting a commercial airliner was not as remarkable a fact as it would have been only a day earlier, for one result (perhaps the only) of my visit to Saint Sebastian was a diminishment of my capacity for wonder, already weakened by several decades of adult life in the known world before I ever heard of this little land it was easy to call preposterous. Perhaps too easy. Did things make any more sense elsewhere? Or, to be fair, any less? It was true that where I came from you could get more or less fresh fish (allowing for the fact that most of them came by truck, in bumper-to-bumper traffic, from Boston), and not plastic. On the other hand, not New York nor any other American jurisdiction, to my knowledge, had a department of hoaxes, though obviously almost any of the existing bureaus could be, with justice, so labeled. The same might be said with respect to a department of irony, and if you got right down to it, was there not a crying need for a government agency that rose above pedestrian meanness to the grander, more generous view: *viz.*, the vision of human problems as allergies? If the Saint Sebastian of old had been ridiculous, it was not *altogether* ignoble. But the stress must go on the penultimate word, for the country's shortcomings were obvious, and it might be asked whether this had really been a feasible way for human beings to live—though not by one who had ever had occasion to travel by Interborough Rapid Transit.

Derailing such a train of thought, perhaps in the nick of time, Olga appeared with a trayful of glasses filled with a liquid off-puttingly colored in a vermilion that looked as if it might glow in the dark.

"I trust you have an alcoholic alternative," I growled.

"Drink this," she ordered. "It was developed for the Sebastiani space program." She lowered the tray from the back of the seat ahead and deposited the glass on it.

"You can't be serious."

"The project may not have gone farther," said she, "but the orange drink was a beginning, anyway."

"You *are* serious. Do I detect a note of nostalgia? Are you already looking back on the old regime with a certain fondness?"

She frowned and went along the aisle.

I put the glass onto the tray, slid out of the seat, and went forward again, passing Rasmussen, who had taken his place in first class and was, of all things, reading a paperback edition of *The Aspern Papers.* Perhaps naïvely, I could not resist returning to comment on this phenomenon.

"This is disgusting," said he, putting a finger to the cover. "Publishers can't even spell anymore." I confess I have never been able to decide whether or not he was jesting.

I continued unopposed into the cockpit, through an unlocked door; hijackers were not feared on this flight. The first person I saw was old Rupert, the prince's butler. He sat in the co-pilot's seat and wore a 1920's Lindy type of leather helmet, the flaps of which were buttoned under his withered chin, the goggles pushed up on the forehead. He turned and sneered at me.

Crammed into the pilot's place was the stout figure of Prince Sebastian XXIII. He wore a green uniform trimmed with gold. Clamped over his billed cap, World War II–style, was a set of earphones.

Though the noise of the engines was considerable up here, Rupert was audible, though he seemingly spoke at no more than his normal volume.

"Go away," said he. "His Royal Highness is engaged."

At this the prince turned. "Wren, old chap! Welcome aboard. I'm afraid we'll have to pig it as to food until we reach New York, but I did manage to bring along a few bottles of Bollinger, a pound or two of sterlet, a cold grouse, and some other things my cooks were able to put in the hamper before they were packed off to become refrigeration mechanics."

I had an odd feeling of disequilibrium.

"Sire," said Rupert.

"Can't you see I'm speaking to Wren?" Sebastian asked in annoyance.

"Sire, we are losing altitude."

"Then pull us up, you old dog."

"But where, sire, is the joystick?"

Sebastian shook his head at me. "The ancient sod hasn't been in an aircraft since the Fourteen–Eighteen War."

"Which side?" I soon had cause to regret my question, for the airplane continued to descend, at an ever steeper angle, yet the prince answered me at length.

"The Central Powers, I'm afraid. But you see, we were surrounded by them, and the Hungarians, who could not whip anyone else, would have been only too eager to punish us if we had not declared ourselves their allies. My grandfather made the necessary decision but of course had to pay the price at Versailles: our so-called empire was dissolved. On the other hand, this was no more than a formality, for our only overseas possession, claimed for the Crown by the Sebastiani explorer Giovanni Dori in 1611, an unpopulated island very near the magnetic North Pole, had long since proved to be only a flat iceberg and, unbeknown to the geographers, had melted during one unusually warm winter. Fortunately we were ignored by all the major powers during the Second World War, though it was touch-and-go at one point, when Marshal Goering sent a team of emissaries to inspect the pictures in the royal collections. Luckily for us, Germans have no taste in art: they soon went away and we were not molested."

"Sire," Rupert said again, but in the same tone of gentle impatience, though I was about to scream by now.

"Haven't you watched me at all, you fool?" Sebastian asked. "One simply pulls back on the wheel!"

I sighed as the old retainer clutched the device before him. In a moment the leveling-off could be felt.

"Of course, he was never much of a pilot, I gather, and was said to have crashed our only airplane on his solo flight. It was not repaired while the war was in progress."

"Highness, how is it that you can fly this airplane?"

"I did such things when I was younger," said he. "I raced cars and boats and could fly any aircraft. All this is in the royal Sebastiani tradition, like sodomy."

"Pardon?"

"I've been deposed now," said the prince, chuckling. "I'm not obliged to be a bugger anymore." I confessed I did not understand. He explained: "I no longer have to take measures against creating bastards, you see?

"Nor need I now get married!" he added. "I'm a free man, for the first time in my life."

"Is it true you will make a series of public appearances in America?"

He nodded. "Having to make a living is new to me. I was going to send Rupert out to work, but then how could I get along? Tell me, is Rasmussen a good talent agent?"

"He's wily enough," I said. "But tell me, Highness, why did Gregor permit you to leave the country?"

"While Saint Sebastian has for a long time existed on credit domestically, we have of course sometimes been required to use money abroad—for my food and drink, for example. I could not abide the swill eaten and drunk by my subjects. And for the odd piece of machinery—for example this airplane—I have always paid cash, and I get it from my accounts in Switzerland. Gregor would like to have access to that money. I agreed to give it him if I were allowed to leave unmolested."

The airplane hit a bump in the road of wind, and had I not clutched the back of Rupert's seat, I might have tumbled.

Recovering my balance, I said, "But, sir, why would he take your word? Once you're in America, you can ignore him with impunity."

Sebastian looked at me with an expression of disbelief. "My dear Wren, I am a prince of the royal Sebastiani line. It would be impossible for me to break my word. And what of my poor subjects? A scoundrel like that would take revenge on them. If the exalted are not trustworthy, then the world would indeed be a hopeless place."

I was amazed to learn that being a parasite did not disqualify a man from having principles. Whether they would survive in his new life of show business was to be seen.

I was about to say something, probably the sort of banality

with which fate provides us on the unwitting brink of a catastrophe, when an explosion occurred somewhere aft. Perhaps Gregor had had second thoughts about letting us go, having found another means of getting to the Swiss accounts, or maybe there was still another group of the disgruntled who made their case with explosives.

Up in the cockpit I was hurled to the deck as the nose lifted violently, then thrown against the ceiling as the balance shifted the other way. Something or someone was suddenly on top of me. Ungodly noises were being produced, the loudest by myself. All was swirling, then dark, then blazing bright, then fragmented, then in horizontal striations. . . . Enough of this: we crashed.

I found it remarkable that I was conscious all the way down, instead of fainting away as I had always supposed was one's obligation, and that in fact after such a fall I was totally conscious. And had apparently—though only tomorrow would tell, for I bruise easily but slowly—sustained no damage whatever.

True, I had fallen only a few feet. What had obviously happened was that, as is my wont, I had lowered my head to rest on my arms, which were crossed on the top of the desk, to ponder on possible solutions to my persistent problem with the second act of my play. At some point, weary from a day's undercover work at Rothman's Deli, aching from the subsequent drubbing I had taken from the gang of little-girl thugs, I had dozed off, my chair had slid slowly backwards, and I fell . . .

Saint Sebastian, and all that went with it, had been but a dream, if not a nightmare. My home, such as it was, had not been destroyed: I was sitting amidst it at the moment. I stood up. Yes, the dog-eared sheaf I called my play was still on the desk. For the first time I could admit that it was a vapid thing, whereas, judging from the dream, I had untapped riches in my unconscious. Now that the Rothman job had come to an end I was at liberty, with more than ample time to begin another play—about a Utopia that was probably not admirable except, like life itself, by chance, but which, like most phenomena, seemed better when it had receded into the past.

But meanwhile I sensed, from the bleak light that penetrated my front windows, that dawn had come to Manhattan: always the best part of the day if you are awake to see it, for the simple reason that so few others are.

I lurched to the window, in a stride reminiscent of the imaginary McCoy (funny how certain items are retained from dreams), threw up the sash, and a pane fell from the rotted wood and went to shards on the pavement below, which fortunately was deserted, else I should have provided another entry for the local list of deaths-by-falling-object: in winter concrete cornices drop, and when summer comes the air conditioners fall like rain. The sidewalk was otherwise reasonably clean this morn, as was even the gutter: indeed I saw Mr. Rat's whiplike tail as he scuttled away with the last morsel of edible filth. A flock of lugubrious-looking starlings was on the edge of the building across the street. I saluted them and cried, "Hey, you slugabeds! Why aren't you up with the Wren?" As it happened, I was in a uniquely fine mood, for no reason at all, as if responding to a posthypnotic suggestion.

Gee, what a nice place the New York sidewalks would be if most people were kept always at the movies!

But when I went to make that matutinal cup of coffee that forms the bedrock on which is mounted the day to come, my mood changed abruptly. The hot plate was still plugged into the socket that hung from the ceiling, but its coils were quite cold, which meant that they had been burned out or the fuse had blown. The fusebox for all the circuits in this wretched building was in a cellar the door to which was locked to keep, as the super said, surely comprising me in his term, "the assholes out." I could easily gain entrance using the all-purpose skeleton key I had provided myself with from Krachlich's Third Avenue hardware store (which offered a full range of burglar's aids), but the fusebox itself was locked more elaborately. Not to mention that Mr. Rat, his stout wife, and their multitudinous offspring made their home down there and at any moment would be, as McCoy might have said in his vivid vintage lingo, tying on the breakfast feedbag. . . . Funny how one can become attached to a supposititious personage, but then, I am in life a lonely man. I wish I could again afford a regular girlfriend: the incessant bickering keeps one on the qui vive. Almost every day I read somewhere that a bachelor's life expectancy is alarmingly short.

I can't function in the morning without my caffeine fix, I don't care what the doom-crying nutritionists say. Unless I wanted to mix my instant coffee with the tepid water from the lavatory tap, I had to go out to breakfast. I searched my pockets for the money I remembered was not there: I found only a crumpled business card, which I hurled to the desk in frustration. I went through the spare clothing I maintained in a heap on the studio couch, then to the garments that hung on the nails driven here and there into the woodwork. But could locate not so much as a single verdigrised relief of Honest Abe. *Merde!*

I went back to the desk and picked up the card so that I might ball it and fling it cursing, an event from which, like most of us, I get a wan satisfaction, and I glanced at it and—good gravy!—saw the legend thereupon: *Our American Cousin Productions, 1 Shubert Alley, NYC,* a 944 number, and *Norman Rasmussen, President.*

But before I could even begin to reconcile reality with dream, my telephone rang. I answered it warily, and this time heard a tenor voice with a local accent.

"There's supposed to be a bomb in your building. Better get out."

I snorted derisively. "Sure there is."

"Whadduh yuh, *arguing?* Bomb squad's onna way. Get out right now."

"Who are you?"

"Getcherass outa there and you can have my shield numbuh."

"You're a cop?" But the distinctive Celtic-tinged speech of the NYPD, even when the speaker himself is Italian or Jewish, was unmistakable. "All right, I'm leaving. But tell me this, officer: why do people do this sort of thing?"

"C'mon, *willyah?*"

I abandoned my attempt to elicit some judgment on these terrorists, if only a pungent epithet, but I suppose cops say "scumbag" only on TV these days. Alas, I had lingered too long in what proved a vain pursuit: I was still in the doorway downstairs when the bomb went off, projecting me onto the sidewalk, where however my fall was cushioned by the small but firm body of Bobbie, my friendly neighbor streetwalker.

"Jesus, Rus!" she protested, rising quickly and dusting her clothing, a slack suit in a subdued color, with her hands.

I got up slowly and looked at my building. It was still standing, nor could I see any flame or smoke. "It's different from the dream," I said.

"Are you on something?" Bobbie asked, anxiously peering at my eyes.

"A bomb just went off in there! Didn't you hear it?"

"You're kidding. That was a backfire over on Madison." Bobbie went into her purse. "Take a look at my new ad, Rus. How you like the writing?"

I accepted the newspaper clipping and read: "Virgin college girl newly arrived in town. Need quick money to pursue Ph.D., and therefore must sell maidenhead to highest bidder." This was followed by the address of a mail-collection service in Chelsea.

"It's clever, Bobbie, but do you think it will fool anybody?"

"You'll see," she said. "I'll get all kinds of answers. The kinda people who read *Crotch* like stuff like that. The kinda people who go to prostitutes are *romantics,* Rus! If you don't know that, you don't know much."

"Do you ever see any articles in there by a man named McCoy?"

She sneered. "I never look at the front part of that piece of shit. I read good stuff, Rus: Harlequins, Barbara Cartland, you know."

"I guess it was a quixotic question, Bobbie. Looks like you're just getting in from a hard night. How about buying me a cup of coffee?"

"Sorry, I don't buy nothing except for Smoke."

"He's the chap who drives the ornate Caddie, wears the big white sombrero?"

"That's my lover-boy. I hope you don't have no criticism."

"Not me," said I. "He has about him the aura of a Renaissance wit. That's all too rare these days."

"You want to panhandle, you go along Gramercy North. That's where the Jewish doctors are."

"Hey, that's an idea."

She frowned. "I don't know, Rus, sometimes I think it oughta be better than this. But then I think, *Where?*" She shook her head as if to clear it, then sighed, took the ad from me, put it in her purse, and came out with a quarter. "Here you go."

I was genuinely touched. "Gee, Bobbie, that's nice of you."

"What the hell. Support the arts!" She gave me a wink and a smile and assumed a sprightly stride as she crossed the street to her hotel.

The bomb destroyed only the WC on my floor, as it happened, and the super, speaking for the absentee slumlord (frankly, I had always assumed they were the same individual), refused to install another, so long as there was a "perfectly good crapper in the cellar."

An anonymous caller informed TV newsperson Jackie Johansen that the bombing was the work of a group which deplored the detonation of explosives on the premises of persons who had no responsibility for the supposed injustices suffered by the bombers. As there was really no other means by which to attract the notice of the press to this organization, the world should expect more of the same.

I haven't yet got in touch with Norman Rasmussen: I started the new play but soon ran into a problem with the second act.